HARD TIMES

HARD TIMES

by Ostap Vyshnia

Translated from the Ukrainian by Yuri Tkach

Book cover and interior design by Max Mendor

Publishers
Maxim Hodak & Max Mendor

© 2018, Yuri Tkach

© 2018, Glagoslav Publications

www.glagoslav.com

ISBN: 978-1-911414-78-0

A catalogue record for this book is available from the British Library.

This book is in copyright. No part of this publication may be
reproduced, stored in a retrieval system or transmitted in any form or by
any means without the prior permission in writing of the publisher, nor
be otherwise circulated in any form of binding
or cover other than that in which it is published without a similar
condition, including this condition, being imposed
on the subsequent purchaser.

OSTAP VYSHNIA

HARD TIMES

Translated by Yuri Tkach

GLAGOSLAV PUBLICATIONS

CONTENTS

Ostap Vyshnia

1889 - 1956

INTRODUCTION

How many famous humorists can you list? Now limit the selection to those who were writing in Europe in the 1920s. Chances are you did not even need to reach for your pencil. Humorists often suffer from a diminished reputation over time, regardless of how well received and influential they were in their own day. Such is the case with Ostap Vyshnia. Back in the 1920s, Vyshnia was one of Ukraine's most popular entertainers. His newspaper feuilletons reached a wide and appreciative audience. In an era when expressing a wrong opinion could get you into serious trouble, Vyshnia's irreverent satire and hearty jokes on topics far and wide—often politically sensitive ones—gave ordinary folks a chance to enjoy a good laugh and breathe a little easier. The story of his own life illustrates just how important and how dangerous such satire can be.

Ostap Vyshnia (the surname means cherry) was born Pavlo Hubenko on a farmstead near the town of Hrun, some 75 km north of Poltava, in 1889. His parents were peasants and Pavlo was one of seventeen children. By remarkable coincidence, his older brother Vasyl also became a well-known Ukrainian humorist, under the pseudonym Chechniavsky. As a young man Pavlo finished the Kyiv School for Feldshers—that is, emergency and ambulance health-care providers. He began working in a hospital run by the South-Western Railroad Administration of the Russian Empire. When the Tsarist government collapsed and an independent Ukrainian National Republic was declared, he joined the ranks of the republic's armed forces and soon rose to the position of director of the medical division of its Ministry of Railroads. It was at this time that he began to write humorous feuilletons for local papers, often satirizing the various political formations and developments of those revolutionary times. It was he who formulated one of the most biting and well-known epithets about the limited power and effectiveness of the Directory, the continuously retreating government of Symon Petliura: 'Inside the railway car is the Directory, beneath it is its territory.' But his jokes were abruptly cut short at the end of 1919, when Pavlo Hubenko was captured by the bolsheviks and imprisoned in Kharkiv until the end of hostilities in 1921.

With some help from influential communists who were familiar with his humor, Pavlo Hubenko got back on his feet in the early 1920s and established himself as Ostap Vyshnia, one of Ukraine's most popular authors, publishing feuilletons in a variety of newspapers with very wide circulations, including the official *Visti VUTsVK*. These short pieces were also collected and republished in books, usually coordinated around a general theme (village life, urban life, literary life, theatrical life, women's issues, holidays in Crimea, industrialization, travel abroad, etc.). Vyshnia was also active in literary organizations, among them *Pluh* and *Hart*. He contributed to various journals, took part in theatrical productions, and became a pillar of Ukrainian literary life overall. But in Stalin's world, pillars were meant to be toppled, particularly Ukrainian ones. Being a stalwart of Ukrainian culture was a dangerous undertaking. In 1933 Vyshnia was arrested and convicted of anti-Soviet terrorist activity, specifically of trying to assassinate Pavel Postyshev, Stalin's personal envoy to Ukraine and the man most responsible for organizing the Holodomor Ukrainian famine and the anti-Ukrainian campaigns of that period. The charges were ridiculous, but the consequences were real. Vyshnia spent the next ten years in the Gulag, mainly in the mining camps near Ukhta and along the Pechora River in the Komi Republic. Some details of Vyshnia's suffering in these camps can be gleaned from the memoirs of his fellow prisoner Iosyp Hirniak (in his *Spomyny*, New York, 1982). Then, in the midst of WWII, Vyshnia's career took another turn. In December of 1943 he was released. The Soviets were advancing against German armies. Ukrainian nationalists, who were fighting against both the Nazis and the Soviets were gaining adherents among some Ukrainians who were horrified by Stalinist repressions. The Kremlin needed Vyshnia as a propagandist against anti-Soviet Ukrainians, and so Vyshnia was released as a sign that the Soviets were not anti-Ukrainian. But this was a bargain with the devil. Vyshnia had to attack the nationalists, branding them as fascists and Nazi collaborators. The most popular humorist of the 1920s was now obliged to prop up the regime that had imprisoned him, tasked with keeping up the fighting spirit of Ukrainians on the Soviet side, and disparaging patriotic Ukrainians who opposed it. This propaganda was kept up for a while after the war, but then Vyshnia drifted back to his familiar, if somewhat half-hearted, anecdotes about the foibles of the human condition. He still knew how to be funny, but the political straightjacket he was wearing meant the jokes lacked the depth and nuance of his earlier writing. After Stalin's death Vyshnia was rehabilitated (he was officially cleared of the "crimes" for which he had been imprisoned). He died soon afterwards, in 1956.

Vyshnia's humor covers a broad range of subjects, but much of it is based on the familiar premise of presenting something complex through the eyes of a simple, down-to-earth person. In the Ukrainian context, this opened some interesting possibilities. The Ukrainian village has long been a subject of satire. It was such in the works of Nikolai Gogol during the mid-nineteenth century and in Ukrainian realist prose later in that century. The Ukrainian village was often satirized in the hijinks of the modernists in the early twentieth century and even in post-Stalinist Soviet Ukrainian literature. In the works of Ostap Vyshnia, the ultra-modern world of revolutionary Soviet society was readily juxtaposed with traditional Ukrainian village culture. The satire worked both ways. The village bumpkins were hilarious because they were so far behind the times. The urban sophisticates were just as comical because their pretentious posturing was just village foolishness in urban garb. What gave the whole sum of Vyshnia's humor a particular coloring was the traditional ingrained sense among his readers that Ukrainian culture—real Ukrainian culture—was essentially a peasant phenomenon and that all these modern Soviet innovations were just the product of some city-slickers (like Gogol's Inspector-General) trying to pull one over on the Ukrainian peasant simpletons.

This perspective is most evident in Vyshnia's stories on the peculiar topic of Ukrainization. Two of the best-known pieces on this subject are "Chukhraintsi" and "Deshcho pro ukrainizatsiu." The latter appears in this volume under the title "Ukrainian Studies." Ukrainization, which was official Soviet policy in the 1920s, called for a thorough cultural transformation of Ukraine, from a land where Russian colonial culture was dominant and Ukrainian culture was the quaint preserve of an unenlightened aboriginal population to a country in which its native culture was dominant and respected no less than any other. Of course, everyone knew, and developments eventually proved, that Russian bolsheviks had no real intention of allowing Ukrainian culture to be dominant in Ukraine. Vyshnia's humor on this topic was particularly effective because everyone understood how delicate the underlying questions really were. On the one hand, he pretended to teach the colonialists about Ukraine as if they really wanted to learn, while on the other hand he also pretended to explain to the benighted natives what a wonderful culture they really had, as if it might be allowed to flourish. Not only did this maneuver provide an excuse for every kind of ethnic joke imaginable (excepting how many Ukrainians it takes to screw in a lightbulb—maybe because lightbulbs were a relatively recent innovation) but it also created in his feuilletons a politically charged atmosphere that never overstepped or criticized official policy, but nevertheless threw winks and nods to those who understood the true nature of Soviet reality.

Given the enormity of Vyshnia's oeuvre and the breadth of his topics, no small collection of his works can do justice to the diversity of his writing. Translations face additional problems, since so much of his humor depends on linguistic peculiarities, puns, local knowledge, and the many other amorphous qualities of good verbal humor. Yuri Tkacz, this volume's translator, together with its editors are to be commended for their valiant effort to present to the English reader the fine humor and incisive social commentary reflected in Ostap Vyshnia's enduring achievement.

Professor Maxim Tarnawsky
Department of Slavic Languages
and Literatures
University of Toronto

TRANSLATOR'S PREFACE

Ostap Vyshnia (1889-1956) was born in Hrun, Poltava Province, Ukraine. He was educated at the Kyiv Military Medical Assistants School, but his literary career soon took over and in 1919, at the 'mature' age of thirty, he began writing and dedicated his life to journalism and satire.

Arrested in 1933 as an 'enemy of the Soviet people,' he was released from the labour camps ten years later during World War II. Upon his release from the camp, he wrote mainly apolitical stories about hunting and fishing, his favourite pastimes.

The large editions of his books in the 1920s and his daily columns in many newspapers meant that Ostap Vyshnia was very well off materially. However, he directed a large percentage of his income to those who most needed it – poor villagers, widows, and those in financial difficulties. Students turned to him as if he were their own father. For several years, he maintained a boarding house for ten medical students in Poltava.

Because of his great popularity and the respect he commanded, Ostap Vyshnia was able to influence the outcomes of court cases against organisations and individuals. Every day, he received hundreds of letters with requests for help, with grievances against bureaucrats – and Ostap Vyshnia reacted immediately with daily feuilletons and letters to the highest authorities.

His works are notorious for their colourful language, being liberally sprinkled with slang and dialectical words, which he constantly recorded while extensively travelling the country. Vyshnia fervently believed that writers needed to write as the people spoke.

My thanks to Serhiy Halchenko for verifying dates of first publication of the works included here and encouraging me to expand and revise this second edition. Footnotes have been added to give greater insight into events, people, etc. of the time.

Yuri Tkacz

CHAUVINISM

They say there once lived this Frenchman in France. Called Chauvin he was, and he proved his love toward his native land, his fatherland, by some amazingly patriotic deed. After this deed of his, every time someone in France proved their love toward their native land, whether a single citizen or a whole group of citizens, this was dubbed chauvinism. And the people who deserved this label—that is, the chauvinists—bore it with pride.

And everyone loved them!

And everyone respected them!

* * *

I first heard this word used quite some time ago.

This is how it happened.

A concert was organized in the school which I attended. We were also allowed to recite 'Little Russian' works. I was one of the performers of these 'Little Russian' poems, fables and so on. I was still a teenager then. I recall that I recited one of Hlibov's fables called *Musicians*.

And so, at the rehearsal I marched out and trumpeted:

"*Musicians*. A Ukrainian fable by Leonid Hlibov[1]!"

The principal came up to me, eyed me closely, smiled, shook his head and said in Russian:

"My, what a chauvinist!"

At the concert, I now introduced the poem thus:

"*Musicians*! A translation of Krylov's[2] fable *Quartet* into the Little Russian language."

And after that I thought for a long time: what is it, this chauvinism? And why am I a chauvinist?

Back then, I didn't find out:

---

1   Leonid Hlibov (1827-1893) – Ukrainian writer, poet, fabulist, publisher and public figure.

2   Ivan Krylov (1769-1844) – popular Russian fabulist.

"Did the principal ever tell me off?"

"Did he ever make fun of me?"

For he never uttered a single word in reference to this again.

* * *

But now I know what chauvinism is!

I've really felt its effect!

I heard about this chauvinism everywhere, and the words they used! The tone of their voices! And the accompanying gestures!

Whenever anyone mentions this word, I grab at my cheeks and jump back a dozen steps, and I feel as if they're going to splash sulphuric acid in my eyes or shoot me dead on the spot!

But Chauvin, God rest his soul, was revered for this very thing.

Obviously, we are not in France!

* * *

I remember this now, after listening to an interview with the eternally aged and eternally new guardians of our Ukraine: Rakovsky, Manuyilsky, Zatonsky...

They're carrying on about that same old chauvinism again:

"We," supposedly, "recognize Ukraine as an independent unit, but we will crush chauvinism, and we will hang chauvinists, including those that are communists...!"

So, take it however you like!

You can be a Ukrainian, but forget about loving Ukraine!

They'll hang you for that!

And the devil knows why this is the case.

If I say, for example: "My regards" in Russian, I love cabbage soup, sour cabbage, Pushkin, bast shoes, piles of rubbish in a Russian *izba*, calves and lice, and I love singing *Vanka Got it On With Tanka*, and in defence of all this I am prepared to go and pillage, kill, hang, shoot, grab people by the throat, forcing them to sing the same ditties and love the same things as me – then that's not chauvinism?

But if I say "Good-day" in Ukrainian, and I love borshch, Shevchenko, a whitewashed peasant house, and sing *Dear Pale-Faced Moon*, without the need to kill anyone as a result, merely asking them to buzz off to their Iveron icon of the Mother of God – then that's considered chauvinism?

And they curse me for this, and beat me up, and maybe even they'll hang me for this!

They're talking about me!

You can wear those bast shoes on your head, for all I care, and you can not only eat your cabbage soup, you can wash in it as well – it's no skin off my nose. The devil take you! You'll all die russkies anyway! And I won't be going to join you! Because I need you like I need a hole in the head!

. . . .

Yes, I'm a chauvinist!

Let them hang me!

. . . .

01.01.1920

MAKING MONEY

Tell me, who doesn't want his bread and butter?

Oh, we all do!

But we all know that to be able to have a nibble of buttered bread, we first need to have the bread and butter.

And to have the bread and butter, we need to buy it.

And to buy the bread and butter, we need money.

And to get that money we need to earn it.

And to earn that money…

Ah, funny people, that's why there's a housing shortage in Kharkiv, so that you can earn money.

You haven't got any money? Then go and let everyone know that you're a real estate agent. That nobody in the world can get them as good a room as you. Nobody.

That's all there is to it…

And then you'll be in the money and have your own honestly-earned slice of bread and butter.

You'll grin all day long and pray to your God each night:

'Dear Lord! Let the housing shortage last for ever and ever! Amen.'

It's not difficult to call yourself a real estate agent…

And it's only a wee bit harder (and only a wee bit) to find a tumble-down shed in some yard (preferably in an inner suburb, of course)…

And you're set…

You catch (more correctly they catch you) people looking for a room…

You know yourself how many of these people there are in Kharkiv now…

"Need a room?"

"My dear fellow! I've been looking for six months!"

"I can offer you a residence (say 'residence' rather than 'room'). An inner suburb, with a yard, ground floor… Electricity, water and central heating in the building… No bond… You just pay for the area you rent."

"My dear man! Show me!"

"That can be arranged, only on one condition. If you don't like it – three rubles for my troubles…"

"My dear fellow! Let's go!"

You take the person there...

"Don't like it? Three rubles..."

"But you said there was electricity, water, central heating."

"There is... in the building. Go in and see for yourself. I haven't lied one bit... The fact that there's nothing here... I didn't mention that this residence had any amenities... It hasn't."

"It's a cowshed..."

"Maybe a cowshed in your opinion, but in my eyes it's a residence... So hand over them three rubles. You promised..."

. . . .

Bring round half a dozen people each day, and you've earned your bread and butter...

. . . .

Hurry, friends... A lot of people are making good money this way and doing quite well out of it too.

12.2.1926

UPKEEPER OF MORALS

Vaska Lob and I hadn't seen each other for ages.

Once we always rejoiced on meeting, even though we weren't the best of friends...

Fate had first brought us together accidentally. We had common interests and often used to sit over a mug of beer in the *Bayadere* or the *Eureka*.

Vaska was no stranger to any of the pubs, and I wanted to be one of the boys too...

I always had money; Vaska liked beer, and vodka too! In other words, we complemented one another.

Vaska Lob and I often did the rounds of the subterranean catacombs, where he was also one of the boys, and we frequented thieves' dens too.

Vaska broadened my knowledge of the coarse side of life; he drank a lot, ate no less, and in moments of extreme affection, he slapped me on the back and said softly:

"You're so naïve! You're a real fine lad, one of the boys, but you're just so naïve, man... Doesn't matter, you'll learn! Just listen to me."

I liked Vaska... Perhaps because he was a 'one-time actor', maybe for some other reason... I was eager to listen to him.

"Eh, you," Vaska would say to me. "You're nothing much! Now me, I'm an actor! Eh, if only you knew how good I was... There were times I'd come out on stage and sing:

> *Oh why, my dea-rest dar-ling,*
> *Are you not with me tonight?*

"They all simply swooned!"

And Vaska began to sing...

At such moments, the barman would come up, tug at Vaska's sleeve and say:

"Singing ain't allowed here!"

But Vaska always finished off the verse and washed it down with a beer.

"All right, quit pestering us. I've finished!"

And he grew pensive... At such times I marvelled at his forehead... Ah, what a forehead Vaska had! What a forehead! Actually, you couldn't see the forehead for the wave of hair covering it. Peculiarly styled, it seemed to arch onto his forehead, every hair in place, then curved around and raced off to cover his temple, becoming lost in Vaska's small head... But this course taken by Vaska's hairdo, its neatness and small curls at the tips – all this was superb and it covered Vaska's forehead quite artfully... The only way to style hair like this is to wet it, comb it carefully onto the forehead, and then press it down with the palm of the left hand. Then with the sweep of a comb held in the right hand, the hair is manoeuvred in a semicircle toward the temple... Only then are you left with such a hairdo... No other way! And not everyone can manage it... But Vaska always wore his hair this way, and it was the best hairdo I have ever seen...

That was Vaska for you! What a hairstyle! That's why I liked Vaska. Later we went our separate ways. I lost track of Vaska. Didn't see him for three years. Even began to forget about him. But as the saying goes, only mountains never meet...

The other day, I was lying face down on the green grass in the local park, watching one insect bite another's head off on the leaves of an orange dandelion...

As I watched, depressing thoughts passed through my head:

'Why does one insect bite another's head off? And why the head?'

Suddenly somebody whacked me with a stick. I glanced around – it was Vaska...

"Risen from the dead? Is it really you, Vaska?"

"It's me, all right!"

"Where'd you spring from? And why are you here? Looking like that too!"

Vaska stood before me in a new dark-green suit, in gangster shoes and a suede glove on his left hand. He was smoking an *Espero* cigarette. And his hairdo? Better than ever! So magnificent and clearly not wetted down with water, but with hair oil...

"Where'd you spring from, Vaska? What d'you do for a living these days? My, Vaska, you look a real dandy now!"

"Want to know? I'm better off than ever, my friend... In the money, and the job's not that difficult, and interesting to boot... I live off love..."

"Married?"

"You kidding? Me get married? I live off other people's love."

"How's that?"

"Still naïve, I see. Others fall in love, and I make a living out of it..."

"They fall in love with you?"

"Gee, you're thick. They fall in love with one another and I live off them."

"How d'you mean?"

"All right, listen! Only not a peep of this to anyone. I'll let you in on the secret... But no competition, because I'm strict about such things these days... People love one another here in the park. Understand?"

"Not really..."

"Come on, man! Right, so you're sitting here in the park... And a streetcar stops across the road. Couples get off and stroll into the park... As though they're out for a walk. You watch out for their intentions. This is where you need intuition. That I've got. You can't fool me anymore. A couple turns into a side alley, clinging to one another. I follow them at a distance, acting nonchalant. And keep an eye out for where they sit down. I make a mental note of where they sit down, but I don't rouse them straight away. In say ten-fifteen minutes I stroll toward the spot. I walk along and chance upon them... I come up to them: 'A-ah! Such indecency! And in a public place! You should be ashamed of yourselves! People come here for a breath of fresh air, and you put on such a display! All right, come with me to the station! We'll make out a report.'

"Now they become very anxious, of course: 'Come on, comrade, we weren't doing anything!'

"And I answer: 'I'm no comrade of anyone who acts so immorally! Follow me!'

"At this point I put on a stern expression...

"Well at this point, of course, they start to beg: 'But it's all so unpleasant... But...'

"And I say: 'It was pleasant enough when you were carrying on! Come along, let's not waste any time.'

"'But citizen...' they begin.

"At this point you can soften a little: 'In the circumstances, I could fine you on the spot. I've got a receipt book with me. The fine's ten rubles and you'll get a receipt. But I don't want to catch you at it again!'

"Usually they pay up, because you pick on the right people... You take the tenner and write out a receipt. I specially bought a receipt book, see... And I write: 'Ten rubles received for acting indecently in the park...'

"'Surname?' I ask them.

"'There's no need for that, is there?'

"'What d'you mean, no need? I need it for the record.'

"I take them for a ride...

"'Just write down any name,' they beg me.

"'All right, I'll take pity on you. I'll make up some name. Here's your receipt. But let this be the last time! All right, on your way...'

"They scram. And I continue to stroll through the park. In a day, I manage to find around five suckers... Life's not treating me too badly, as you can see. And at the same time, it's a morally satisfying job..."

Vaska rose to his feet and stared somewhere ahead.

"Well, I'll be off! The fish are biting. It's a never-ending job. See you 'round, then!"

And Vaska hurried off. I watched him go and thought:

'There's Vaska for you! A real moralist!'

November 1926

HOW TO IMPROVE YOUR HOUSEHOLD

(Verified by many)

The best way to improve a household is by hard work.

Especially communal labour.

That might be the case in Germany, but in our country people say:

"Don't spin yarns... Collective wealth belongs to the devil."

Let them talk, we'll carry on as our grandfathers did before us.

"Even though I go without bread, I weep alone, my legs are swollen from overwork, my back is bent double, and I'm at the end of my tether."

And communal labour? In a group, there's less work and greater prosperity, but that's communal... Which automatically means it's worse...

But I don't wish to talk about such methods of improving household prosperity: going it alone or in a group, it all still means having to work.

For there are much easier and much more profitable ways...

'Community' ways...

Want me to teach you?

Good. I've been told a lot about them and I've read extensively on the subject myself.

This is what you need to do... Set up a cooperative in your village. It's a very profitable thing... The state and everyone says so...

You call a meeting and begin:

"We need a cooperative! A cooperative!"

And everyone answers:

"We agree!"

"We need one!"

"Let's elect a board!"

The elections take place.

And at this point declare yourself to be the best Soviet citizen and make sure you force your way into the cooperative – straight onto the board.

You're on the board and you work hard. You collect shares, open up a store and begin trading.

Trade well, take conscientious and painstaking care of the business entrusted to you.

And when the time comes for an audit, and they ask you where the cooperative's money has gone, reply:

"I don't have it."

"Where is it then?"

"I don't have it."

"Squandered it?"

Remain silent and don't say a word... If you're very brave, you can venture:

"Yeah, I've squandered it! So?"

Then they draw up an indictment, call a meeting of shareholders and the inspection committee reports to the gathering.

The assembled people say:

"What a sonofabitch! Just what we thought! He shouldn't have been trusted with public money."

You step forward and say:

"Can I have the floor?"

"Go ahead, speak!"

"Respected company! They say here I've supposedly squandered public money. No two ways about it, it was cooperative money and it should be here. But I never squandered it, cross my heart... Forgive me, my fellow citizens, I won't do it again... Don't leave me destitute, I'll try and pay all of it back somehow..."

Everyone is silent.

Then a faint voice rises from the crowd.

"Well..."

"Speak up, man...!"

"Well... I've got nothing to say."

Everyone is silent...

Then from another corner:

"Well..."

And everyone is silent.

Then it's hard to say from where, but someone begins softly:

"Ah...let him off! What can we make him pay back?"

And then:

"Yeah, let him off!"

Then louder still:

"Ah… let him off!"
The chairman of the meeting asks:
"So what then? Do we let him off?"
"Yes!"
"Enter it in the minutes."
They pen it in.
You bow for the 'last' time.
"Thank-you, respected ladies and gentlemen."
And that's all there is to it…
And then two weeks later you build yourself a shed, buy an old nag and a few other similar things…
You don't blow the money on drink, of course, because your household won't show any improvement then.

———•———

Apart from improving your household through a co-operative, you can also improve it quite well through land distribution.
You are elected authorized agent for land distribution, you collect money to pay for a surveyor, for organizational expenses, and then:
"Forgive me."

———•———

Maybe there are swamps near your village.
Then land melioration really helps…
Set up a melioration company, collect membership fees, and then:
"Forgive me!"
Even, for example, take such an organization as MODR[3]…
You might ask, does helping revolutionary fighters abroad have anything in common with agriculture in our villages?
It has, apparently…
Collect money for MODR, and then:

---

3   MODR – *Mizhnarodnia orhanizatsiia dopomohy bortsiam revoliutsii* (Intenational Organisation to Help Revolutionary Fighters), a mass organisation whose aim was to provide material and moral aid to the victims of fascism, and reactionary and tsarist terror. Existed 1922-1947.

"Forgive me!"

———•———

Our working peasantry is ever patient and ever gracious – just say 'I'm sorry' and all is forgiven.
And later they'll stop and eye your new cowshed and say:
"Ah, the sonofabitch. 'Cooperative', hah!"
And they'll waddle off, tapping away with their walking stick…

. . . .
Forgive me!

07.07.1925

THE BEST AND SUREST WAY
OF BECOMING RICH

Don't bet on horses. Because far too often horses bring disappointment. The damned beast struts past you before the race, tail in the air, and neighs and prances, as if to say:

'Bet on me!'

You place your bet on him, and he drags his feet for two days to cover the mile...

He runs along and cries:

"Let me go, jockey! My word. I'll beat them all..."

The jockey, of course, guides the horse along, for he too wants some bread and butter occasionally...

Well, you don't win... The jockey wins... He's like that.

Cards are a dubious means of making money too. Sure, you can win, but then you may have to 'play back'[4]. And this already spells great unpleasantness for the wife and the mother-in-law, for it is too cold now to queue outside prison with food parcels.

But there *is* a great way.

A shop. Any old business[5].

Open any sort of business, sit down and trade!

No one comes to you, business is bad. You're going bankrupt.

Bankrupt, because your wares are expensive. Because the public's purchasing power is small.

You feel awestruck.

But there's no need to grieve.

Grab a sheet of stiff card and write on it in large letters:

'30% discount! Only during October!'

---

4   i.e. go to prison.
5   During the New Economic Policy of the 1920s small businesses were allowed to flourish in the USSR.

Hang this announcement in the window or on the door. Smile, enter the shop and shout to the sales assistant:

"Hand me the price list!"

Take the price list.

"Serge cloth? One ruble... Hm..." And where there was one ruble, you write two.

And so all the way down the price list...

A man in the street passes by and sees the sign.

"Thirty percent!" He grabs his wife, his kids, his money, and rushes to your shop:

"I'd like this... and this... and this..."

And you say to him:

"Yeah! There's a sale on... Hurry... Because later..."

When he leaves, you sit down again, smile and read about the fleecing of city and village folk...'Cause you know only too well, that only... etc.

And here you are, making consumers happy as anything. Offering them thirty percent off...

So there!

. . . .

Recently I met a friend. He'd bought a pair of galoshes from a cooperative shop... They glistened brand-new on his feet.

"Hello," he said.

"Hello," I replied.

"What if I were to belt them? Just go and whip them hard?"

"Whip who?" I asked.

"All those traders..."

"It's not civilized to go whipping people..." I said. "Really, how can you do such a thing? Whip people?"

"I think it's unpleasant too! But I heard somewhere that if you belted an old dog hard enough, you could teach it new tricks..."

"Well, that's a dog, perhaps..."

01.11.1923

GUARD THE STATE'S WEALTH

Well, we've raised the dust with a serious campaign...

A fight for thrift, reduction in spending and economy...

So that each and every copeck is spent wisely, so that the nation's wealth is not squandered, so that people no longer point at a cooperative chairman or some such and say:

"Whistled it away, the sonofabitch! Blew all our money!"

Yes, that's the sort of campaign we've embarked upon...

What does it mean, this campaign?

Well, it's like this...

You've probably heard about such great perks in our economic institutions as 'shrinkage', 'shortage', 'wastage'[6], travelling allowance, overtime, advance and so on.

You buy, for example, some leather or sugar for the village store...

You buy a thousand pounds, but by the time you get it to the store and it has lain about for a while, you find it has 'shrunk' or 'evaporated' or 'wasted away' by a hundred pounds or so...

So what do you do with the damned sugar?

It wastes away, damn it. Shrinks quickly, crumbles away so fast, that it makes your hair stand on end. And then the inspector comes along:

"Where's the sugar?"

"It's wasted away."

"What do you mean, wasted away?"

"Ye gods, it's gone and wasted away! The devil take me, if I'm lying... I even knelt before the sack and begged it: 'Please don't waste away, old chap...' But it keeps on wasting away... And we've already lost a hundred pounds..."

The same goes for all kinds of travelling allowances...

You go into town to buy some material... In town it's forty-five copecks a metre, but by the time you get it to the village it's one ruble forty-five a metre.

---

6 Slang terms used by the man in the street for stealing of goods and produce by government employees.

"A bit expensive."

"Eh, expensive. Go and find out for yourself whether it's expensive or not. Of course it's expensive... There's accommodation in town to cover... And transportation back... Yes, it's expensive... And it shrunk about thirty yards by the time I got it back here."

"What do you mean, shrunk?"

"Just what I said. They sell wet material... And a wet yard is a long yard... I was carting it back, and the sun was really scorching, and the yard shortened... And now there's thirty yards less... And you say it's expensive..."

* * *

That's what things were like... And they haven't changed...

So let's have no more of this...

It's difficult, but there's nothing to be done – we must act...

Because things have begun to waste away so much, that if we don't knuckle down, we'll waste away ourselves.

8.4.1926

HARD TIMES

"Is this a joke?"

"What are you referring to?"

"This decree here from the National Labour Commissariat on work discipline in the public service..."

"It's no joke!"

"So I have to roll up to work at ten on the dot?"

"On the dot!"

"What if I sleep in?"

"What do you mean by 'sleep in'?"

"What if my constitution is such that I happen to sleep in every day?"

"Don't know..."

"The bastards! First purges, then layoffs, and now – start work at ten on the dot!"

"Well don't come to work on time then."

"But it says here they'll fire anyone who breaks the rules."

"Well, come on time then."

"On time! It's easy for you to say 'come on time'... What's this world coming to?"

The work day lengthened by half an hour...

No time for a proper lunch, no time for a decent stroll down the corridor. Sit at your desk all day long! And work, work, work!

"All day long!"

"The bastards!"

And my female colleague dashed off, waving her hands about in disgust.

* * *

Times have changed all right!

What's all this leading to?

Just think, such discipline in a Soviet (a Soviet!) establishment!

This is nothing short of penal servitude!

Tell me then, how do Soviet work conditions differ from tsarist times?

How?!

And what about all those who rant and rave: 'Yes, I serve the state! Of course I serve the state. After all, I have to make a living somehow! Only I seem to be running around more than serving!'

What, I ask you, are they to do now?!

They'll burst into tears!

"Have mercy on us! Soviet establishments – and yet such rules!"

These are hard times! Cruel times!

Farewell, corridor!

Farewell, mirror!

Farewell, my dear toilet!

14.02.1925

AN ALTERNATIVE

These are hard times, citizens. Hard and complicated times. And the worst part of it all is that life continues to grow more complicated…

Your head spins, you grab it between your hands, and sturdy thoughts slither down the furrows of your large brain:

"What's to be done?"

They've begun to catch people in earnest…

Take a bribe and they take you in…

Whether you're a treasurer, an agent, a farm manager, a deputy rep or the rep himself – it makes no difference: they show no mercy!

Whether you've taken the money because of 'strained financial circumstances', or whether the money's simply been used for 'banquets', or whether, moved by the most humane of intentions to help homeless children, you lost it at roulette, cards or on horses – they still show no mercy!

It makes no difference whether you rendered great services to the Revolution, or might do so in the future!

What heartless souls there are now…

People say they'll show no mercy whatsoever!

It's said they'll show no mercy even in cases where you swear at the trial that although you have rendered no special service to the Revolution, you feel that in the event of a global counter-revolution you'll capture Hindenburg single-handed.

Do not pin your hopes on anything… And when you appear before the court, don't say:

"Forgive me, citizen judges, I'll take Perekop single-handed!"

Because they'll show no mercy.

How complicated life's become…

Gone are the good old days, when there were great positions that allowed you to take bribes…

Alas, no more!

These odious times have put forward an alternative: don't take, or they'll come and take you!

The only thing left for bribe-takers is to put the Soviet regime to shame for 'borrowing' the eighth commandment from Moses:
'Thou shalt not steal!'
Though I doubt if it will have any effect.

25.9.1925

THOSE UKRAINIAN PEASANTS!

"Can you imagine? A *muzhik* in dirty pants, and without a tie, comes to see me in the Justice Office and forces, simply forces his way up to my desk! 'Can I have a certificate?' he says. Appalling! Simply appalling, I tell you. So I told him:

"'Wait in the hall, please, comrade!' Can you imagine, he continues to stand there and even considers whether he should go or not! The cheek! I'm up to my ears in work... And here I have to converse with some peasant. My hair was out of place, you know, I could see my nose was shiny, and the *muzhik* continues to stand there – I couldn't even powder myself. It was a fight and a half to get rid of him.

"Such sudden urgency. I mean, if it had been something important... He was only appealing about some land... You know, the stuff that turns to dust when there's no rain. They sow pearl-barley and macaroni on it, I think. And he calls it a pressing matter."

"Yeah, they've got a real cheek. Imagine. I had a similar experience. Sitting there, cleaning my nails, and this peasant rolls up and drawls in Ukrainian:

"'Listen, comrade, how are things? When are we leaving? And will you be issuing us with tickets, and how, and when? There's no time to sit around, the millet still needs to be sown.'

"Really made me mad, you know. Such a peasant! Really – I doubt if we could survive without their lot... But at least talk like a human being, you imbecile. But no, he launches into Ukrainian. Country bumpkin! I put him in his place of course. 'Speak to me in Russian,' I said to him. 'You can talk to your peasants in your own 'lingo', but speak the universal tongue with me.' Well, did he ever blow up...

"'Bread,' he says, 'you understand that in Ukrainian! Yet when we come here, you act dumb!'"

"Yes, real impertinence."

1920s

MISFORTUNE

And so, an agricultural credit association was formed in the village. They hung out a sign and elected a board of directors. And the members of the association told the board:

"Work hard! Work hard, so we can lead a better life! Because credit is a big asset to a villager!"

And the board said:

"We'll work hard! Because credit is a big deal to villagers! The Soviet government knows this too and provides large sums of credit. Don't worry, we'll work hard!"

"Work hard, comrades. The government may be playing its part, but don't you fall asleep. Show some initiative, for without independent action we're both done for..."

"Don't worry, comrades, that's what we're here for, to show initiative."

And the board set to work.

At the board meeting, the director says:

"I'm off to town tomorrow! I have to explore a few avenues, do some soliciting and running around. For he who does not sow, does not reap."

"All right, agreed."

"One of the board members can go to the regional centre. We must keep busy."

"All right, agreed."

Just then the accountant came in.

"Don't go, chaps. You need to give me a hand!"

"What's the matter?"

"Reports need to be written."

"What reports?"

"Well, two copies each to the Bank of Ukraine, the Regional Country Union, the People's Commissariat of Finances, the Ukrainian Country Bank and the Regional Executive. And each is demanding detailed balance sheets, information on fixed capital, loans, etc.

"Besides this, the PCF also requires a complete list of association members. And there are five hundred of them... That's fifteen pages of writing."

"All right, we'll give you a hand, and then we'll be off!"

"I don't think so…"

"Why?"

"Because next month'll be here by the time we finish! Time for the monthly report…"

"So when do we get down to business?"

"Don't know, chaps."

"Well, you can all pitch in and help, while as head I'll go off…"

"You can't."

"Why?"

"Because inspectors are coming."

"What inspectors?"

"Tomorrow from the Provincial Bank, the day after that from the Regional Country Association, then the NCF inspector, next a special district commission, after that a general inspection, and then the man from the Ukrainian Country Bank…"

"Well then, after they all finish, I'll be on my way…"

"I'm afraid you can't, because after the UCB inspector there's the man from the Provincial Bank."

"Back to square one then?"

"Yes, back to square one."

* * *

So the board sat down and burst into tears.

3.3.1925

SEARCHING KHARKIV FOR A TRACTOR YARD

I've known for a long time that tractors are very useful.

And I've seen them too.

But I never thought I'd be running around Kharkiv looking for a tractor.

I haven't got any land and I'm no state farm manager. But look for a tractor I did…

I was walking down Sverdlov Street, tractors far from my mind…

Going on my merry way.

I noticed two fellows walking up ahead of me. They looked around searchingly and slapped their sides… They stopped passers-by, asked them something; the passers-by answered with a flutter of hands, the fellows shrugged their shoulders, looked around and scratched their heads…

I caught up to them.

"Hi," the two greeted me.

"Hi," I answered.

"Tell us, please, perhaps you know where the tractor yard is around here?"

"Tractor yard, you say?"

"Yeah!"

"What do you want the tractor yard for?"

"We bought a tractor and now we want to collect it."

"Where d'you buy it?"

"Over there! Straight ahead, then a little to the left…"

"Did they issue you a receipt?"

"Yep! We've even paid for it."

"Let me see…"

"Here…"

A receipt from the Kharkiv Provincial Bank for a *Fordson* tractor from their warehouse…

"Didn't they tell you where the warehouse was?"

"They said it was somewhere round here."

"Have you been to the Machinery Trust on the corner there?"

"My word!"

"And?"

"They said it had nothing to do with them."

"Did they direct you where to go?"

"Nope, they knew nothing about it."

"Come with me."

I went to a telephone and rang the commercial section of the Provincial Bank:

"Where are your tractors? Where's your warehouse?"

"One moment, I'll find out."

Three minutes later:

"We don't know. Ask at Industrial Trading. They'll be able to tell you where our warehouse is."

"Have you got their address?"

"One moment..."

After two minutes or so:

"On Katerynoslav Street, up near the square... There's a sign outside. D'you know where the square is?"

"Sure!"

"Well ask there!"

"So, I need to ask at Industrial Trading where your bank's warehouses are and they'll tell me?"

"Well, yeah!"

"Thanks..."

And then I bid the fellows:

"Follow me. We may be in luck. I seem to have hit on the right track..."

"Lead the way, we've had it!"

So off we went.

"Finished threshing?" I asked them.

"No! We're waiting for this tractor... We were hoping to drive it down today and make a start early tomorrow morning..."

We reached Industrial Trading.

"Where are the tractors here?"

"We haven't got any."

"What do you mean? The Provincial Bank sent us here!"

"You need the tractor department!"

"And where is it?"
"On the second floor!"
"Let's go."
The second floor...
"Where's the tractor department?"
"Over there!"
We went 'over there'.
"Where's the tractor department?"
"Over there!"
We finally found it...
"These fellows here are looking for a tractor. They paid for it at the Provincial Bank. So where's the tractor?"
"Hasn't arrived yet!"
At that point I gave up... I simply quit. By Christ, I got the hell out of there.
"I really must be off. I'm late for work! Work it out yourselves, comrades."
"Thanks for helping!"
I turned and fled.

28.8.1925

OUR QUALIFIED GRADUATES

A young man graduates from the Chernihiv Agronomical and Industrial Technical School... Majoring in agronomy...

After graduation, he goes, for example, to the village of Veresoch.

He goes full of desire, full of gusto and energy to help the ignorant peasant in his uncultured work with such rich, such cool, such black, such generous, such fertile, and such-such-such soil...

And his cart is filled with desire, and his cap is bursting with desire. In short, he is all desire...

He arrives there...

"Hi, I'm an agronomist, comrades... I've come to help you improooove your soil... With the help of science, fellas..."

"G'day! Good thing you came... We're in dire need of someone with your qualifications... Because the soil needs tilling!"

"Well, then... Unharness my stallion here, and toss him something to munch on...!"

"There's no need to worry about that...!"

"Eh, Mykyta! He says to unharness his stallion. Hear that? He's got a mare, and it's in foal too! What a nitwit! Some stallion, my oath: it could even possibly foal tomorrow... If only we had stallions like these... My, what a lamebrain!"

And the next day...

"Well then, comrades, shall we start? What month is it? July! Harvest time... Well, then! Let's start with the millet! We'll harvest the millet first, then the buckwheat, then the oats, and then we'll do the rye. Ever cut 'Paris Green'? It's high time, high time! Otherwise it'll become too ripe! Do you cut it with a cockle cylinder or a hoe? It's better with a cockle cylinder[7], you know. Much faster. By machine, after all... In the time you tire of swinging a hoe about, you can clean up a

---

7   A cockle cylinder is in fact a machine used to separate grain. The graduate, fresh out of technical school, knows nothing about agriculture, confusing the names of breeds of horses with breeds of cattle.

hundred acres… Especially if you've got good Simmental or Schwitz[8] horses – goes like a breeze then! Ardennes bulls are good too, but they must be well-bridled, so they don't damage the machine…"

"What…?"

"And then remember not to delay with the clean-up… Straight after the harvest you have to plough in the stubble, so that you can sow the winter maize in August… Have you got a broadcaster? There's nothing like a broadcaster for maize… Field crops like wide open spaces… And don't forget to clean the seed, 'cause you never can tell what things have infested it, all kinds of silkworms and moths… When I look at your orchards, I can see everything's covered in smut[9] too… You've neglected your farms… Very much so… There's meadow butterfly on your cattle, your pigs have foot rot… You need to shoe them… An unshod pig is no pig at all: its hooves grow out and crack, and it neighs so dolefully then… But we'll put all that right. I didn't finish technical school for nothing!"

. . . .

"Listen, mister comrade! Go back, and quickly, to wherever you came from… We've even harnessed your stallion in foal for you… And don't look back! 'Cause Kindrat over there's already fingering a hefty stick… And he's a very hot-headed type of fella…"

. . . .

The fine young man leaves… Full of gusto, full of energy, and thinks:

'Ignorance! Ah, what ignorance!'

13.7.1923

---

8   Simmental and Schwitz are in fact breeds of cattle, while Ardennes are a breed of draft horse.

9   Smut is a fungal disease of cereals, not fruit trees, and meadow butterfly attacks vegetables, etc..

MY MERRY GALOSH

The other day I caught a bus from the railway station to the centre of the city. As we moved along, I stared outside onto the footpath. Mud everywhere, of course, since it was autumn and raining. Mud to the ankles…

We drove past the Rubber Trust[10]… A queue outside as usual – some two hundred, maybe a thousand people… The workers and the idle standing in line. All forming up for galoshes…

The bus continued on its way and I became engrossed in thought…

Suddenly something exploded with such hysterical laughter under my seat, that it made my leg shake… I glanced down, my right galosh was guffawing…

Laughing its head off!

Cracking up with laughter.

"Hey, what's the matter?" I asked.

"Queues outside the Rubber Trust!" chuckled my galosh and burst into fits of laughter.

"They're queueing because it's autumn… I mean, where can you set foot now without galoshes?"

"They should set foot in the market," said my galosh. "There's enough of my kin there to build a dam!"

And my galosh began to tell me about its 'road to Calvary'…

"I arrived in Kharkiv from Moscow, old chap. They put me in the Rubber Trust warehouse. We lay there for a while. Then somebody shouted:

"'Take them to the cooperative store!'

"They piled us into a lorry and took us to the Central Workers Cooperative Store. When we arrived there, the co-operative chairman called out:

"'Hang up a sign that there are no galoshes!'

"So they hung a sign up…

"We lay there in peace for a while…

"Then they began to throw us about quietly, look us over and whisper:

---

10   Government organization producing and selling goods made of rubber.

"'We need sizes nine and ten! You've only got thirteens and fourteens. No great demand for them.'

"They sorted us, packed us into a box and carried us off with a smile:

"'Now we can make some money!'

"Next thing we knew we were at the market. Lying there, brand spanking new.

"And whereas we cost three rubles before, now we were selling for six!

"We were merry, so were our owners... Though we did feel a bit queasy whenever somebody banged us against the table and bellowed at our owner:

"'May the devil twist your insides into a knot!'

"And so I lay there till I fell into your hands. And now it seems so funny: the Trust and the Cooperative are sitting on the galoshes, while the consumer is going without."

And my galosh started to chuckle again.

"Cut it out," I said, "my leg's trembling!"

"Shut up!" said my galosh. "Or I'll burst my sides. Then you'll be up for another six rubles or you'll have to join that queue!"

"Laugh to your heart's desire, my dear, only please don't burst."

And my galosh laughed for a long time...

It wasn't at all funny, but I kept my mouth shut...

31.10.1925

A JACK OF ALL TRADES

A red sign with a hammer and sickle hangs outside the village council, a small house with an iron roof, surrounded by trees... In a park... Not your ordinary park, but a prince's park. The house was also owned by the prince once.

Now back to the village council...

The village head, Nalisny, works in what was once the elusive prince's study. Nalisny certainly isn't elusive. And next door, where they say the lady of the manor had her boudoir, the villagers read books and thrum the prince's grand piano – there's a reading room in here now...

Once upon a time the prince owned this village... Now it's ours... The park, behind the park, in front of it, and over there – it's all ours...

As they say, anything is possible under Soviet rule...

The village council administers the village up there on the hill, this park and the flowery fields beyond it.

Four thousand five hundred people fall under its jurisdiction...

The village head and the secretary sit at their desks all day long. They are on the job when the sun just peeks over the horizon, and they're still there as the sun falls below the horizon.

Sitting at their desks writing...

Writing and talking...

There's no ten to four job here, it's before ten and after four.

There are no appointments. The door creaks open:

"G'day!"

"Can you tell me how much tax I owe?"

You search the files...

"Tell me, how are things with that meadow behind Khoma's plot of wheat?"

You tell him...

"Could you perhaps marry us today?"

You marry them . . .

"Grandpa has kicked the bucket."

You arrange the funeral...

"God sent us a baby girl yesterday!"
You do the christening...
You stand in for the priest and the deacon...
And all in this small iron-roofed house.

* * *

How many People's Commissariats are there in the capital?
How many commissions?
How many committees?
And all of them governing, God bless them...
They all write:
'Notice to all provincial...'
In the provincial departments, the memos go to the appropriate section. The section goes scratch-scratch:
'Notice to all district...'
In the district offices, the memos go to the appropriate section. The district people scratch out:
'Notice to all rural...'
In the rural offices, the memos go to the appropriate section. And the rural people write:
'Notice to all village...'
And here that avalanche from all those sections spills out before the village head or the secretary in one enormous pile. And the head sits in that small house at his small desk and eyes the pile of paper...
In the village, he is the commissar for education, land, health, internal affairs, justice and finance... He is the local representative for the state's industries, he is the trust and the syndicate.
He must oversee the harvest, the weeding, the ploughing... And in each case he is 'personally responsible' and everything must be done 'without delay'.
Ye gods, the village council receives some thirty-five letters each day...
And we haven't even completely liquidated illiteracy... When we do, we'll show them!

5.7 .1925

HOW SAD

It's winter...

No sowing, no harvesting, no reaping to be done, no grain to thresh...

No need to tend to the cows, no rounding them up each night...

Plenty of sunflower seeds... Hooch... *Russian Bitter*... Dances in the evening...

Fill your pockets with sunflower seed, cock your hat, roll yourself a cigarette, grab the accordion, go down to the cooperative store, get a bottle of grog, down it and stagger along the street, singing merrily.

Kick away at gates and hammer on windows!

Eh, the single life!

A girl hurries past, you send her flying head over heels!

An old bag runs past, you trip her over!

Oh, what a life! Oh, what joy!

But no, some stupid official has to go and spoil it all with his 300 ruble fine for hooliganism!

What's life going to be like now?

So you have a few drinks and stay at home?

A few drinks and off to bed?

Without tarring any gates[11]?

So do you go off to the clubhouse?

Or the reading-room?

Or the village hall?

Oh, Lord! Lord Almighty!

How sad! How boring!

29.10.1925

---

11 Tarring a gate was done to show the whole village that the owner's unmarried daughter was no longer a virgin.

UKRAINIAN STUDIES

1. Especially for Russophiles

A few popular lectures in Ukrainian Studies, especially for those people, who have hitherto not been interested in the topic, are not interested in it and will never be interested in it...

What is Ukraine?

Ukraine is "that native Russian land – that Little Russia, where abundance reigns"[12]...

It stretches across the open spaces of Kharkiv, Poltava and Chernihiv *gubernias*, Novorosiya and the Southwestern Region.

This is Greater Ukraine. Besides this, it also consists of Red Rus', then Subcarpathian Rus', Hungarian Rus', and, in general, all other kinds of Subjugated Rus' regions.

Thus: Little Rus' + Red Rus' + Hungarian Rus' + Subcarpathian Rus' + Subjugated Rus' = Ukraine.

In this here world there are also: White Rus', Finnish Rus', Lithuanian Rus', Caucasian Rus', Turkestan Rus', Siberian Rus', but these are not part of Ukraine.

Ukraine's capital is Kyiv.

It acts as "the mother of all Russian cities".

The father of Russian cities is yet to be found, but he definitely exists somewhere.

He fled promptly, having begotten heaps of little towns.

The uncle of Russian cities is Chernihiv, the fiefdom of Saint Fedoska Uhlytsky[13], whose oak tree still helps relieve people of toothache. The oak

---

12   First part is a commonly used Russian phrase for territory Russians consider as theirs from time immemorial. The last words are the opening lines from Aleksei Konstantinovich Tolstoy's poem "You know the land, where abundance reigns".

13   Feodosiy (Teodosiy) Uhlytsky (Saint Feodosiy of Chernihiv), (1630s – 1696). Canonized in 1896.

wood is used thus: a piece is bitten off the oak tree with the afflicted tooth and is chewed until it becomes a mush.

Bila Tserkva was a close relative of Kyiv, while Poltava was its midwife.

For Kyiv's christening, Zhytomyr baked *knysh* pastries, while Vinnytsia made moonshine.

The main river in Ukraine is the Dnipro, which has also been dubbed 'the cradle of Russian glory'.

Ukraine's population is made up of Little Russian topknots.

They are all called Solopiy[14]. They all wear wide pants.

They blabber in peasant lingo and sing very few Russian songs when they dance the *hopak*.

Their peasant lingo is now the official language of the country and everyone must know it.

It's very similar to Russian.

The Russian word for "trust" is "*trest*" and the Ukrainian word is "*trest*" too.

Syndicate is "*syndykat*" in both Russian and Ukrainian.

"Director's fees" is "*tantiema*" in Russian and in Ukrainian.

So that there is hardly any difference and those to whom I am dedicating these Ukrainian studies will find learning the language not difficult.

Only be mindful that the word 'percent' (*protsent* in Russian) is not *protsent* in Ukrainian, but *vidsotok*. Although the meaning is exactly the same.

But words like 'stock exchange' (*birzha*), gold (*zoloto*), gold coins (*chervintsi*), bank notes (*banknoty*), sterling (*sterling*), dollars (*dolary*) are identical in Russian and Ukrainian.

So, don't be scared of Ukrainization.

II. For Bona Fide Ukrainians.

And these are lectures for those who were overinterested, are overinterested, and will continue to be overinterested in Ukraine.

What is Ukraine?

---

14   In Ukrainian the name literally means 'a very inattentive, slow-witted person'.

Our Mother Ukraine is a state stretching from the Bay of Biscay to the Gobi Desert or Shamo[15].

It was established 5000 years before the Autocephalic[16] Lord God created the world.

The first man was called Ostap (not Vyshnia, because they didn't have surnames back then), and his wife was black-browed Halya.

During the Great Flood it was Hetman Doroshenko who built the ark, not Noah, and who rescued seven pure Ukrainian couples and one sour-cherry pip, which then gave rise to all those cherry orchards in Ukraine; the dog Brivko, who then fathered a whole breed of authentically Ukrainian Ryabkos, Lyskos and Lapkos; several skeins of yarn to embroider shirts, a piece of linen, a pot to cook borshch in, some gut to make sausages, a mace, various regalia and the notes to 'Away, Away, Gray Geese'...

After that, Egyptian pharaohs lived in Ukraine, then Henry IV, the Bourbon dynasty, the Pope and Ivan Kalita. All these were Ukrainian leaders, a fact which the Russian historian Ilovaysky[17] hid from us in his time.

The Dnipro River in Ukraine is the largest river in the world; it starts at the Mississippi and flows through the Gulf Stream into the Blue Sea. In the past 'Titanics' navigated the Dnipro, but those thrice-damned Russkies imbibed most of our Glorious Dnipro River water and it seems to have grown shallower.

But that's nothing: we'll squeeze that Dnipro water out of the Russkies with the help of the French.

The language in Ukraine is the best, the sky is the best, the soil is the best, the railways are the best, and the people are the most civilized in the world.

To the north of Ukraine live those thrice-damned Russkies, who feed exclusively on Ukrainians.

To the east are the Poles, a very fine, brotherly people.

And beyond them lies Europe, just waiting for Ukrainian culture to appear.

So these are some brief notes that you won't be able to find in any book on Ukrainian history, and of which I wanted to remind you, so that you don't forget.

27.04.1923

---

15 Chinese for 'desert'.

16 Tongue in cheek comment, that Ukrainians consider the only true God to be theirs and thus He must be Autocephalic.

17 Dmitriy Ilovaysky (1832— 1920), a Russian historian.

THE CLUBHOUSE

The youth of Ivanivka made merry at the village evening get-together, till suddenly out of the blue someone blurted out:

"Let's go to the clubhouse!"

Even the youth of Ivanivka occasionally want (though very rarely) to go to the clubhouse!

And so they headed off...

And came up to the clubhouse...

And went in...

And knocked on the door...

"Who's there?"

"Us young people! We've come for some political education, to liquidate our illiteracy, and generally speaking, to have a good read... Because we're still pawing each other in the evenings, just like before the Revolution. Our hands hurt, we want to give them a rest!"

"You can't come in right now. The village head's just taken off his shoes, Ivanko's scratching his heels and a woman's come to gossip with his wife... So there's nowhere to sit... And in the reading-room the secretary's granny is washing Oryshka, who's shitted herself... And the wash tub's in there, so the clothes can soak overnight."

"Well, bring us out a few books then!"

"Sorry, the books are covering the cream right now... Come 'round tomorrow. We'll have finished the washing and churned the butter by then, and the clubhouse will be free!"

"Well, off we go, boys. On with the pawing."

And off they went...

* * *

They should have given the head of the village council and the secretary a good hiding instead.

Bashed them about the head.

8-10.03.1925

CHOOSE ONE OF YOUR LOCALS

The head of the Poltava Provincial Executive Committee received the following declaration:

> *To the ProvExeCom Head*
> *from pensioner Ms P.M.D.[18]*

DECLARATION

Please marry me off to an educated Russian communist with a view to create a famous man for Russia and communism.

[signature]

17/XII 1924

The declaration was forwarded to our newspaper...

While we consider the intention of the declaration commendable, unfortunately we are all extremely overburdened with our present duties... We are about to publish an illustrated journal, the newspaper *Red Youth*, and *The News* is expanding too...

There is no time, comrades, to see our own wives for weeks at a time, let alone for 'a view to create a famous man'...

Our thoughts on the matter are that the spinster's request should be acceded to, but please make do with 'local talent'.

3.01.1925

---

18   *The News* has full name and address in its files. *O.V.*

TRUE CHRISTIANS

There are those who complain that our people have forgotten God and the Gospel...

Nothing of the sort.

In Katerynoslav[19] Province, not far from the former Zaporozhian Sich of the Cossacks, there is a settlement called Virny.

Recently the residents of Virny bought a schoolhouse in the neighbouring village. It had been a parish school. They began to move it. But the local priest began to fret and asked that the toilet be left behind for him...

The men replied:

"We'll only take the boards away, and you can have the hole in the ground and what's in it."

In true Christian tradition:

'Share what you have with your neighbour...'[20]

The people are still very religious...

12.7.1924

---

19 Now Dnipropetrovsk.
20 Hebrews 13:16 is in fact: 'Do not neglect to do good and to share what you have, for such sacrifices are pleasing to God.'

TRADING IN AIR

There's an island in Katerynoslav[21] where the tired inhabitants used to go on public holidays to soak up the sun and warm their sides…

They went and went… And no one minded… There's as much sunshine as you like, and fresh air too…

And then…

Some wretches decided to cash in on this.

They set up a table, put a person behind the table and took a *hryvenyk*[22] from anyone who wanted to soak up the sun.

A workman asked:

"And if I haven't got a *hryvenyk*?"

Our answer is:

'Then you won't be able to warm your sides…'

Come to Kharkiv – they don't sell these commodities here yet…

. . . .

Who needs this?

Whose brainchild was it?

And they devised a sneaky method too… You don't pay for lying in the sun, but for walking through the park…

The park is sweet nothing, they say: just bushes and stumps…

Comrade Lenin once said:

"You must learn to trade."

But he didn't have air and sunshine in mind.

12.07.1924

---

21   Now called Dnipro.
22   A three-copeck coin.

MARKET DAY

I

Well before the crack of dawn a voice booms outside:

"Wake up! Time to go to market!"

Veremiy Vasylevych has rolled up to the schoolhouse with his pair of oxen...

One has to set off early to market, 'cause it's twenty kilometres away, and one still wants to get there in time to find a good spot, park one's cart properly and take in all of the day's events.

Some have already left that evening with their oxen. They graze their cattle along the way to make them nice and plump for market. Then they'll cost the earth.

"Gee up, my little darlings!"

The little darlings run along, tails swinging, rear passages rumbling, livers, lips and teeth jumping about.

"Gee up! Will you look at her! Just look at her!"

'She' is running along the edge of the field, wheat spikes scratching her 'snorer', and so 'she' stops and starts.

Then comes a crack of the whip and: "Look at her go! Will you look at her go!"

...Off to market.

———•———

Dawn is here. The sun pokes out its sleepy muzzle, whips its rays out across the meadows, the steppes, the orchards and fields...

And as far as the eye can see, right up to the woods over there, the road is covered in carts... Pulled by horses, oxen and cows... Wagons, carts and cartlets... Heaped with hay and straw... Laden with chickens, tied-up sheep and bleating calves struggling to get up... And the carts are followed by foals, weaners, and young cows with calves tied to their tails.

"Hey! Haw! Gee! Giddy-up!"

Off to market.

And still they come, and come, and come...

The road's turned into an enormous motley snake, alive and twisting, slithering out of sight into the woods...

Neither its head nor its tail is visible – it stretches from deep in the wood to beyond that hill over yonder.

Our cart jumps out of the flow, sometimes to the right, sometimes to the left, rattling over clods of earth, rustling through grass...

"A good day to you, Petrovych! Off to market too?"

"Of course! And a good day to you!"

"Taking your Dutchie along?"

"O'course!"

"Bursting with milk?"

"That she is!"

"Well don't get diddled!"

"We'll take things as they come..."

A piglet squeals from a cart, lashed to the side ladder with rope... Kicking about, the poor thing is unaware that it is no longer an ordinary piglet, but has become an object of the domestic budget...

. . . .

"Eh! What a 'gentleman' you've got there!"

"The 'gentleman' is in a cage... He's an enormous, well-fed boar... The cage on the wagon towers like a dome on a church, and the 'gentleman' inside is sprawled out, grunting nervously...

"How much for the 'gentleman'?"

"Ask me at the market..."

. . . .

A river of village carts flowing along... To market!

People here from Manylivka, Brovary, Vasylivka, Popivka, Fedorivka, from the settlements...

And they keep coming, and coming, and coming...

After crossing the Psiol River, this motley snake, this colourful ribbon spills out onto the market-place, mingling with those people already encamped here, and voices call out to horse and cow alike:

"Whoa!"

Arrived at last...

. . . .

The market-place fills with a mass of humanity, cows, oxen, horses and sheep, spreading out in all directions, reaching the banks of the Psiol River on one side, and everywhere else extending to the stalks of rye standing heads bowed, waiting for the scythe to do its work...

Tents and marquees are already up... Pitched the day before, in good time, they stand like bulging blisters in the bustling speckled crowd...

The market place is clogged...

Clogged with wagons, carts, buggies, horses, cows, sheep, oxen, calves, pots, dishes, chickens, wool, sacks, hops, lambskins, fabric, boots, sweets, gingerbread, *kvas*, beer, vodka, scythes, combs, skins, belts, skillets, hemp, scarves, linen, tar, kerosene, rags, shirts, skirts, rugs, brushes, barrels, horns, singlets, wax, honey, treacle, roach, herring, wheels, treadles, glass, eggs, *zapaskas*, *plakhtas*, pies, bacon, meat, sausages, fried fish, sacking, trunks, nails, hammers, pigs, hucksters, Gypsies, horsedealers, people, children and blind beggars...

...And everything is stirring, breathing, smoking, talking, shouting, cursing, lowing, bleating, neighing, ruminating, yawning, oinking, snorting, swearing, smelling, stinking, ponging, cackling, clucking, slapping hands, pumping accordions, playing violins, reciting, drinking *kvas*, eating salted fish, belching, hiccuping, husking sunflower seed and riding merry-go-rounds...

And towering over all this are thills, thills, and more thills...

Carts have raised their thills and holler: 'We're sel-l-l-ling!'

Over there a cloak screams from a thill:

'Here we are!'

A sieve over there calls on its kind to come forth:

'Come this way!'

And over there a wheel spoke is caught on an upright shaft:

'Here we are...!'

. . . .

And they keep coming, and coming, and coming...

"Gee, I said! I said, gee!

"Gee! Gee! C'mon, gee, may those wolves not gobble you up!"

"Gee there! Gee there!"

"Whoa!"

Caught on a yoke...

"What devil is driving you onto other people's yokes? Can't you see I've stopped here?"

"Think you're the only one here?"
"And you are?"
"No, I'm not alone!"
"Couldn't you pass around me?"
"Think you're the only one here?"
"And you are?"
"No, I'm not alone!"
"I told you to keep left… What the devil made you go for my yoke?"
"Think you're the only one here?"
"And you are?"
"No, I'm not alone!"
"Back! Back! Whoa – back!"
"Rushing about the market like it was an open field!"
"Think you're the only one here?"
"And you are?"
"No, I'm not alone!"
"Hey, left I said!"
Unstuck at last…

———•———

A constant din…

And above this din, like an accompaniment to some grandiose organ, the monotonous recitations of the beggars.

Give us alms, my dearest daddy,
Give us alms for the sake of Christ!
Give us alms, Christians with righteous souls…
Alms, mother dearest, give like Christ…
Give alms like Christ, merciful father.
Give us alms, you souls that are saved,
At least one of you merciful souls…
Give us alms as you pass by, hearing our words,
Whatever you have in your hands, mother dearest…
In memory of parents, family and the departed…
Saving the soul inside your sinful body…
…Give of the fruits of your toil,
Of your brute strength…
Give of the fruits of your toil,

Of your hard labour...

And the accompaniment of the crowd buzzes on and on, at times becoming a wild roar...

Now it has died down and spreads across the market-place in a low rumble...

One minute, two, three...

And suddenly right beside your ear:

"Rags! Bring your rags here, old women! Rags taken in, money shaken out! All your rags here! Bring your rags here, old women!"

"*Kvas*! Fizzy, icy cold, sweet as honey! Get your *kvas* here!"

"Bet a ruble, win two! Gather round! Gather round!"

"Red wins, black loses..."

. . . .

The din rises again... Becoming deafening once more...

The ruddy blind man's basso profundo voice strains and breaks. Violin in hand, and with a blind female partner beside him, he tries to outdo the hubbub with a sad psalm.

And night came then to the Messiah,
Bearing scented oil in hand
Came sorrowful Marias
With unease in their hearts...

The market is buzzing...

Horses are prancing about, hucksters are yelling, girls are roaring with laughter, the merry-go-round is spinning...

The organ on the merry-go-round wheezes and whistles, spewing forth onto the stalls, the carts and the calves a song about a merchant who:

Fell in love with all his heart
Ready to make a fresh start...

And to this wheezy song young men and girls, and children turn round and round with joy...

"A fiver! Only a fiver!"

The market...

. . . .

II

Why do oxen bellow so tragically and hopelessly at the market?

When a person enters the cattle section, he is met with:

"Moo-oo! Whaa-ah! Ba-ah! "

A tawny or grey beast, a speckled or a bay one stands there, looks about and, without warning, lets out a:

"Mmo-o-o-oo!"

"Wa-ah!"

"Ba-a-ah!"

Are they just supporting the general din in the market, or is it because they don't want to change hands? Maybe it's something else entirely?

"What about the sheep?"

They are such small things, but when they bleat, it sounds like there's a radio inside them... Abrupt and piercing...

"B-bah!"

Like a rifle retort...

Just the one single word, 'B-bah'.

There's every imaginable type here.

Tawny, spotted, bay, grey, black, mousy, bald, with spiral horns and hornless...

And there are bulls, and oxen, and steers, and weaners, and cows, and heifers and calves...

Standing beside carts, and yokes, and in men's arms, and beside stakes...

A lone stake in the ground, a cow beside the stake, a tail beside the cow, a calf beside the tail...

And its owner nowhere to be seen... A solo-cow...

Only when someone comes up and pokes the cow in the side with a stick, and asks:

"How much is this one asking?"

Then a straw hat or a cap appears from nowhere and says to no one in particular:

"Fifty!"

. . . .

And what oxen there are here!

Well, maybe they're a little smaller than the bridge across the Lopan River!

Standing beside a cart, ruminating and thinking their oxen thoughts...

What's it thinking, that grey one over there with the large horns?

It must be thinking something!

Maybe it has its own philosophical thoughts?

Maybe it too saw a tractor somewhere in Kremenchuk and now looks melancholy, and thoughts crawl along the furrows of its brain:

'So I'll become completely obsolete soon?'
And offended, it bellows:
"Moo-oo-ooh!"
The grey oxen thinks its grey oxen thoughts.
Thinking away until someone unknown to it comes along, flicks it with a whip and asks the owner:
"How much for this pair of turkeys?"
"Well, I'm asking three hundred!"
"Three hundred, you say?"
"Yes, three hundred!"
"It'll take too long to count the money!"
"How much then, to make the counting easier…"
And the haggling begins…
They pull the grey beast by its tongue and open its mouth wide, take it by the horns, and feel its throat, measure it from hoof to mane with a whip handle, tug at its tail, feel under the tail…
"Three hundred, you say?"
"You heard right…"
"Walk 'im up and down!"
"We can do that…"
The grey fellow is untied from the cart:
"Hey!"
"Slowly, slowly! Don't rush him!"
"No need to look… Goes like clockwork…"
"My grandmother went all the way to her grave on such 'clockwork'!"
"No need to carry on…"
"So how much, if I mean business?"
"I'm talking business!"
"No, come on, talk business!"
"I've already told you, three hundred!"
"You wouldn't give them away for a hundred and eighty, would you?"
"Go take a hike!"
"And I will too!"
"You do that!"
"Don't turn away! I'm offering you good money!"
"I can see they're not crockery shards!"
"It's good money! Don't think…"
"I'm not!"

"How much then? Will two hundred do?"

"No! If you want it so much, let's make it two hundred and eighty! There!"

"Two hundred and eighty... Praise the Lord!"

"Let's!"

"Take two hundred?" (Slap!)

"Two hundred and eighty." (Slap!)

"I asked, are you ready to take two hundred?" (Slap!)

"Come on, talk business!" (Slap!)

"Then speak business." (Slap!)

"Just take a look at the bullocks! They're crucians, not bullocks. They look like children in the yoke! Little sweets! Grab them by what you like, crawl under them – they're as tame as a baby sister! Wouldn't touch a child, and you're carrying on about 'two hundred'!"

And they pull the grey beast by the tail again, open its mouth, try its throat, feel under its tail, grab it by the mane, pat its neck...

They walk around it and look it in the eye...

"Have mercy! Two hundred and twenty!" (Slap!)

"I won't go below seventy-five!" (Slap!)

"No?" (Slap!)

"No!" (Slap!)

"Hold onto 'em then...!"

"And I will...!"

And the stranger moves away from the grey beast... He shoves off, and then calls from behind the fourth or fifth cart:

"Will you take two hundred and twenty?"

"No!"

"Better take it, or you might take a turn!"

"Doesn't worry me..."

And the grey beast remains standing beside the cart, thinking its oxen thoughts, until someone starts up again:

"How much for these sookies?"

"Three hundred!"

And so on, and so forth...

Maybe the grey beast will go home, maybe it'll go to another farm, or to another village... Or maybe it'll end up with that 'gentleman' with the long thin flail, wearing a jacket and a golden ring on his finger – and then the grey beast will become Beef Stroganoff at the *Tivoli*. The grey fellow stands there and ruminates.

And there are cows everywhere... Those cows that 'flood you with milk'...

"How much for this jerry..."

(The jerry is grey, her udder a leathery pouch smeared with dung.)

"Sixty!"

"Get real!"

"Up yours!"

Brief, but decisive... They haven't reached an agreement.

. . . .

"How much d'you want for this madam?"

"Eighty!"

"Not asking much..."

"Just take a look – she's as pretty as a picture!"

"Yeah, that's true! But some girls have a nice mug, you could drink water off their faces, but when you look down there, they're a bit on the hard side!"

"It's up to you..."

"Yeah! You ought to ask less!"

"Yeah!"

. . . .

"How much for the *child*?"

The *child* is a rounded black steer with tiny horns.

"Twenty-seven!"

"Let the child grow some!"

"And I will!"

. . . .

And they pray, and cross themselves, and slap hands, and send each other to the devil, and oaths fill the air...

Buying and selling... Selling and buying... Trading...

And everywhere one turns:

"Moo!"

"Wah!"

"Bah!"

. . . .

...Stalls... A street filled with stalls...

Stalls with drapery, boots, *kvas*, sweets, gingerbread, dried fish, herring, belts, iron...

Red flags flutter over the stalls.

Red flags above small signs.

'Ostapivka Consumer Association'...

'Popivka CA'...

'Fedorivka CA'...

A stream of humanity flows between the stalls – there's no room to push your way through.

Material for pants, shirts, skirts...

"Is it strong?"

"You couldn't tear it with your teeth."

"How much?"

"Thirty-five..."

"That's a bit rich!"

And they tug at the cotton, try their teeth on it, and consult, consult, consult...

There are more scarves over here, more blouses and vests.

It's a woman's paradise....

"You here too? G'day!"

"Good health to you!"

"Making a skirt?"

"No, a shirt for Fedko..."

"How much?"

"Thirty-five..."

"I've just gotten my kids a *fairing*..."

The *fairings* are covered in colourful wrappers, with tails at both ends, so enticing...

"How much?"

"Three copecks each..."

"E-eh!"

"I've got some at two for a copeck! And these are five a copeck..."

"And these are twenty a copeck! Get these – they're sweet and good."

"Let me have some!"

. . . .

Cast-iron pots clanging, scythes ringing, heckling combs clattering...

"How much for this hackle?"
"Buying a hackle too, friend?"
"My oath!"
"Take this hackle here, good woman!"
"It's a bit small... I need one which I can use for squashing lice and for spinning too..."
"Take this one! You can kill a tiger with this one!"
"I want it to be smooth as well..."
"That one's forty!"
"Take a hike!"
"Grab the smaller one, it's cheaper!"

. . . .

Old men milling around the scythes... Clank, clank, clank...
Grinding one against the other...
"Something's not quite right about them..."
"What do you want then?"
And again:
"Clank! Clank! Clank!"
Taking half a day to choose a scythe...
"Clank! Clank! Clank!"

. . . .

"Eggs! Eggs here! Come here for fresh eggs!"
"Rags! Rags! Old women – bring your rags here!"
"Grab a chook with you! Chooks here!"
"*Kvas! Kvas* here! Only here and in Moscow!"
"...Ruble down, win two!"
"Last of the dried fish! Dried fish!"

. . . .

> *Give us alms, my dear father,*
> *Alms for the sake of Christ . . .*
> *Alms, God-fearing and righteous Christians...*

Organ wheezing... Violin howling...
And the basso profundo with the thin indifferent soprano beside him:

> *The bird soared in the air*
> *Flying ceaselessly*
> *Flapping its wings*
> *Praising the Lord. . .*

. . . .

Market day!

. . . .

III

"Ca-arrre-foo-ool! Careful! Careful!"
"Gee-up! Gee-up!"
...Swish! Swish!
"Eh, my Arab!!!"
"Gee-up! Careful there! Careful!"
"Don't hit them! Hey! Slower, slower!"
"Stop tugging!"
"Go get!"

. . . .

Horses... Mares... Colts... Foals... Hell...
Everyone with a whip...
Whips come first here, then people...
Whips whistling, cracking, lamenting...
One hears:
"I-hi-hi-hi!"
"Eeeeeeh..."
"Trrr! Trrr!"
And – swish, swish, swish!
Here they are conducted along, raced past, harnessed up, paraded by...
Here 'Pray to the Lord!' and 'Go cross yourself!'are somehow nervous, impetuous, frenzied...
"Keep talkin'!"
"Kee-eep talkin'!"
And this *talkin'* is not simply a word, but a mad cry...
"Keep talkin'! Go on, talk!"
Here they slap hands furiously, with sheer exertion, taking a good wide swing, so that you fear your hand will fall off any minute and roll under a wheel!
"Keep talkin'! Go on, you, keep talkin'!"

. . . .

"Why are you looking at the teeth?! Look at her! Just look what she's eating! Brushwood?! Brushwood! Grinding away at it like a mill..."

"Well..."

"What are you 'welling' about? Eh? May the Lord strike me dead, if she eats anything 'part from straw... And you 'well' me..."

"Look at her... Look how she walks! How does she walk? Watch her heels! Shows all four heels... Look there, not at her teeth..."

"A bit gaunt though!"

"No two ways about it, she's a spent nag. And you thought she had it milk and honey! If you were driven hard for twenty miles and then put on a diet of straw – would you jump for joy?"

"Well..."

"You can chop her into pieces! Load her up with a tonne, and she won't bat an eyelid! And you're checking out her teeth? Well?!"

"Well, how much d'you want for her?"

The fellow is holding his white nag by the reins. Its hind leg is tucked in, lower lip sticking out, it's dozing...

"Gimme thirty!"

This means give the horse and thirty rubles on top for taking it...

They begin haggling...

"Take it *swappo*..."

Swappo means exchanging one thing for another...

"What d'you mean, *swappo*?! Look what you're holding there... A beggar! And you want *swappo*..."

The 'beggar' swishes its tail indifferently...

A Gypsy runs up, opens its mouth and pulls out its tongue:

"Lord have mercy, it's just as bad in here as in its arse!! And he wants *swappo*... Come on... Talk business! Come on!"

"Want a fiver?!"

"That's money too!"

Hands slap together with a crackle, hats fly to the ground, obscene curses fill the air, the horse runs along, whips crack, a loud yell pierces the ears:

"Watch out!!"

This comes from the main horse avenue, where the Gypsies and horse-dealers have gathered...

Carts stand in a row, earth is banked up near the carts, and the horses are positioned with their front legs on the mound to make them look more imposing, straighter...

Any old Arabian shoots past two walls of burning-biting whips, and galloping up to a cart, breathes heavily...

An inexperienced farmer can be swindled so badly here, that bringing his new horse home, the man screams:

"Help!"

And takes the animal to another market, where people swear by the Lord and cross themselves before him, run past, tear past, pull off his hat, strike his hands, point at the horse's teeth, legs and mane...

The farmer looks, crosses himself, slaps hands and says:

"Twenty-five!"

He takes the animal home, arrives, takes a good look:

"Help!"

He goes to a third market...

Then the farmer is left without a horse and without any money...

When a farmer is offloaded a 'roarer' here, there's laughter and grief...

A 'roarer' is a horse with a disease of the lungs or some such... So that when it's stationary, nothing is wrong with it. But take the horse for a ten-mile jog and it begins to roar (choking!) like a bull...

"A showy bit of a horse, and I didn't pay much extra for it... Cheated the fellow," the farmer thinks.

Hops onto his cart and sets off for home at a fast trot!

Reaches home!

"Whoa!"

And the horse answers:

"Wa-a-ah!"

"Oh, help! Whoa!"

"Wa-a-ah!"

"Oh my God!"

"Wa-a-ah!"

. . . .

There are no ordinary geldings here...

Here we have:

"Lion!"

"Eagle!"

"Thoroughbred!"

"Kestrel!"

"Breeze!"

"Squire!"

There are no ordinary mares here, only:

"Birdie!"

"Storm!"

"Cliff!"

"One-of-a-Kind!"

Take Lion for example...

"This is no ordinary gelding, a true Lion... Just you look!"

When Lion walks along, its hind legs look like a pair of dividers, something slimy is oozing from one eye and its ribs are already poking through its skin.

"Careful there!"

Lion jogs along, dragging its hind legs...

And here's Eagle...

As it walks along it limps on its left hind leg:

"Ruble-twenty! Ruble-twenty!"

"Sure, the gelding's limping. Exhausted by the trip! But the horse is good! A real peasant's horse! An Eagle...!"

Eagle's left hipbone is a quarter of a hand higher than its right...

Eagle...

Birdie has been harnessed for a ride. Birdie has a buckwheat coat, with joint inflammation, thin as thin can be...

There's an utter abyss under Birdie's tail – she's been drawn in so much. Birdie is bridled. Her tail is tied up at the very stump. So that everything is on view! How she walks! How she runs!

"Giddy-up!"

Six souls on the cart.

"Giddy-up!"

Lash!

Birdie's abyss answers with a spurt.

Giddy-up!" (Lash!)

Spurt!

Poor Birdie has 'the wets'. 'The wets' is a disease horses have (nervous or something), that when you whip them, they urinate involuntarily.

"Whip!"

"Spurt!"

"Look! A real fantail! Giddy-up!"

Poor buckwheat mare. She too neighed happily in the meadow once!

. . . .

Eagles, Lions, Squires, Breezes, Birdies, Cliffs and Storms race about here...

Stung by merciless whips, they gallop along, stumble and pant...

. . . .

"It's a stallion! Too much trouble with them. If he was gelded..."

"Too much trouble? Stallion? Go geld yourself! Don't look there, look at his chest... He's a veritable mountain!"

. . . .

"This is a gelding?! I'm looking for a stallion!"

"A stallion?! But there's so much trouble with the bastards! You have to watch their every step. Look at the gelding! It's a real horse, not some pissy dog!"

"The gelding's fine! But why's it got 'buckwheat' all over its coat? They say the blood's botched when the coat goes like that..."

"Utter rubbish... The mare was grey, the 'procreator' buckwheat... So there's your buckwheat... He's got grey from his mother, and now his father's colour is coming through... From the procreator... There!"

. . . .

"Bought a mare yet, Petrovych?"

"Sure have..."

"How much d'you give for her?"

"My red nag, plus eleven rubles, half a quart of vodka and a hundred and eighty pounds of next season's wheat..."

So how much did the mare cost, tell me?

. . . .

"Ca-a-areful there! Ca-a-areful!"

"Giddy-up! Giddy-up!"

"Hey there! Hey there!"

...Horses galloping, Gypsies running, Gypsy children scurrying, dogs barking under Gypsy wagons, whips cracking, foals neighing, stallions grunting.

'God' and 'mother' curses fill the air...

. . . .

The market...

. . . .

IV

...The sun is scorching hot!

Belting down as if it was in league with the whips...

Piercing you with its rays, pouring its rabid heat into your breast, stomach and head...

You quaff *kvas* and crawl under a cart, hurry over to the Psiol River and, ripping your clothes off, dive into the water and splash with the horses, cows and oxen...

People are leading animals to and from the Psiol by the reins and on tethers:

"Off to wash them! Off to water them!"

The tired animal, stunned by all the noise, wades into the water, stops, has a few guzzles and keeps the flies at bay with its wet tail...

And each tail sends a spray across the Psiol no worse than a priest's aspergillum.

In the market-place, overlooking the Psiol, the trading continues...

Actually, there is more noise than trading here...

Because:

"Well, how's it with the oxen?"

"Quiet. No buyers... So we bid among ourselves... Some money from the side and business would take off..."

"What about the horses?"

"Same thing there. The Gypsies and horsedealers over there are palming off cripples, while the farmers have brought theirs out, and still not a bite. Farmers are strapped for cash just now, it being close to harvest time..."

"There are no 'serious' buyers. They're all putting it off till autumn... When the animals are sold off before winter, when they'll be cheaper, then everyone will snatch them up..."

....

Fish is going well... Textiles are a bit slow... Kitchen utensils... Bric-à-brac... Wool is going well. Lambskins are being ripped out of traders' hands. Chooks are being grabbed from baskets... Eggs... Hemp...

There is less noise here and more business...

....

The sun's rays are becoming a little slanted...

Things are quieting down...

Under carts, under drays people gather to snack...

Corks from *Russian Bitter* fly high...

Bottles stand stopped up with rags – filled with home-made brew...

This is a *mohorych*, vodka drunk to conclude a sale.

"Let's drink!"

"May your bay mare run swiftly and bear foals easily!"

"Let it be so!"

And the clear liquid bubbles from bottle to mouth and spreads through the veins, and men grow red, eyes become bleary, voices grow louder and hands move faster.

Tipsy...

. . . .

Some are already heading home.

Horses and oxen are being harnessed...

"Home..."

The motley snake is crawling away from the Psiol River into the steppes.

. . . .

The stackyard comes alive...

This is where the horses are... Horses are untied from carts and led onto the road between the carts...

The stackyard...

"Eh, red foals, who's first?!"

"Who wants a light-bay horse?"

"Who'll take the grey?"

"Watch out!"

"Giddy-up! Giddy-up!"

"Watch out there!"

"Keep talkin'! Keep talkin'!"

Slap! Slap! Slap!

The stackyard is filled with 'mother' curses. There are quite a few now who have had several drinks... Sealing their purchases with drinks.

Slap! Slap! Slap!

"Wa-a-atch out there!"

The final agony...

Another hour and the market-place is quiet...

The stackyard is empty... The horsedealers living nearby are harnessing their horses... Those living further away are making themselves comfortable for the night.

The market is still on tomorrow!

The merchants pack their wares away. Night falls... Fires flicker near the Gypsy tents, supper is being cooked...

The blind beggars are silent... Only the merry-go-round organ keeps imploring 'Vanka':

> *Kick the vodka habit, Vanka,*
> *Let's go out and work*
> *We'll stuff our pockets full of money*
> *Every single Saturday...*

The organ grows silent...

Evening is here...

And then it's night...

A dark, black, gloomy night...

On such nights, Gypsy tents are lyrical and Gypsies are poetic... On such nights, sorrowful Gypsy songs fill the air:

"A-a-a-ah! A-a-a-ah!"

"A-a-a-ah!"

A song as drawn out as the steppe...

And listening to that drawn-out, sorrowful song you forget that black-eyed Halya is dying of hunger, and her father, Yashka, is drunk by the tent, heaving foul curses at her mother...

Such is the night...

Black Gypsy children, who flash bare bellies and wheeze under tents and wagons, resemble the progeny of the free steppe inhabitants. A thin exhausted Gypsy woman over there is burning lice on the fire and a young voice is singing ardently:

> *Tusa-tusa-tusa*
> *My kamam chy-cho*
> *I love you ardently*
> *Ekh! Tusa-tusa-tusa...*

Dark night... Enchanting night...

Perhaps it's the night, or the stars, or... an empty stomach which brings the young Gypsy Vanka to his feet from under the wagon, and he shouts:

"Halya! Something more lively!"

And then the girl's lungs emit a fast chant:

> *A-ta-ra-ra-rai-ra!*
> *A-ta-ra-ra-rai-ra!*
> *A-ta-ra-ra-rai-ra!*
> *A-ta-ra-ra-rai-ra!*
> *A-ta-ra-ra-rai-ra!*

And Vanka patters around the fire...

He moves as if he is floating through the air, fire licks his bootlegs, and his chest explodes with:

"Ekh! Yeah! Let's go!"

And Vanka launches into a freestyle Gypsy dance, and his hands beat time on his bootlegs:

"Tra-ta-ta!"

Dishevelled people jump from wagons and, scratching, gather round the fire, clapping, shrugging shoulders, stamping feet...

A-ta-ra-ra-rai-ra!

A-ta-ra-ra-rai-ra!

"Ekh! Let's go!"

"You show 'em, Vanka!"

Vanka floats around the fire and only his feet whiz about, while his figure is like a bow string...

"Ekh! Ekh! Ekh!"

Vanka kicks with his heels... Kicking in ecstacy, kicking with gusto, as if his bitter fate was stretched out on the ground around the fire, as if his poverty was lurking there in the knotgrass, together with his hungry days and sleepless nights, his young wife's exhaustion, the dirt of his small children, the whooping-cough of his inflamed and festering hungry horses...

"Ekh! Ekh! Ekh!"

"Rrright! Rrright!"

Heels! Heels! Stamp on that poverty, that bitter Gypsy fate!

The fire is out...

...The marketplace is quiet...

...The marketplace is empty...

Stalls stand silent in the darkness... Gypsy tents lurk grey...

You lie stretched out in the middle of the marketplace with a small pile of hay for a pillow, an enormous fine black sieve overhead, perforated in millions upon millions of places with stars...

...A horse neighs.

A whip cracks...

A Gypsy swears...

A dog barks...

Silence... Sleep...

"...Whoa! Stop!"

Blink twice and the sun's rays are already picking away at your teeth.

"Time to get up, lads..."

Again they ride about, giddy-upping, heying, geeing, hawing, whoaing, cursing and crossing themselves...

The second day of the market...

Bells ringing in heads, feet dragging, eyes screwed up...

"Home! Are we leaving soon?"

"Yes!"

"...Go-o-o-o on! Go-o-o-o on!"

Slap! Slap! Slap!

And bells echo in heads:

"Clang! Clang! Clang!"

Harness him up! We're heading home!"

Mares running along, a red foal skipping behind them.

Home!

Finished marketing...

A light breeze blows in their faces, airing the market's din from everyone's head.

Giddy-up!

. . . .

"Carrreful! I'll squash you! Eh! Mother-mother-mother!"

"Christ-Christ-Christ!"

Glance back to see a cloud of dust rolling down the hill toward you, and a voice pierces the air:

"Mother-mother-mother!"

Alyosha rolling home... Floating in an inebriated mist from sealing all those sales. Kneeling on his cart, reins in one hand, a whip in the other, and lashing his pair of bay horses...

"H-harr! I'll run you all down! I'll run all you bastards down!"

"Slow down, Alyosha, or you'll really run someone over!"

"Look out! Alyosha's coming! Alyosha will run everyone down, brother, he's the best horsedealer in the region! Brother, Alyosha's a civilised dealer! Alyosha's the smartest among you! Come on, find a smarter guy than me! Aha! Brother, you can't! Alyosha can out-do anyone! Yeah! See? H-harr! H-harr, my hearties! Out of my way!"

Alyosha falls back in the cart, the horses slow down, Alyosha tips forward and hits his forehead against the front of the cart, the horses dart forward, Alyosha reels back, the horses slow down, Alyosha crashes forward...

"H-harr!"

The reins are taken away from him, Alyosha is subdued on the cart.

"On your way, slowly..."

The 'best horsedealer in the region' drives off, waving his right hand about.

"I'll diddle you all! See this pair of horses – I'll drink them away. Anyone keen to? Turn off, we'll drink everything away! Pull over! Let everyone know how Alyosha makes merry! H-harr!"

"Sit tight, Alyosha, or I'll tie you up!"

"H-harr! You know who I am? I'm no bloody fool, brother! I'm no bloody fool! Lay your peepers on my horses. D'you ever have such horses? H-harr! What horses! They're not just horses, they're a joy!"

Alyosha roars with laughter, teetering on the cart.

"Stop! Whoa! Stop, I tell you, 'cause this bay one is sick! He'll die! Stop, don't rush, 'cause the horse's sick! He's a good horse, but he's sick..."

Alyosha bursts into tears, and tears flow in streams, falling in dirty drops onto Alyosha's blue shirt.

...Alyosha has fallen asleep... His forehead resting against the coupling bolt, Alyosha is asleep on his knees...

You look and you're not sure who'll do who in: will Alyosha's forehead smash the iron coupling bolt, or will it crack Alyosha's forehead open.

The 'civilized horsedealer' is returning home from market...

His pants are wet and a stream dribbles from the cart...

"Alyosha, the cart's afloat! You'll drown!"

"Eh?! H-harr!"

He wakes up and collapses again...

Alyosha has finished marketing...

. . . .

Time to head home...

But even the next day the head reverberates with:

"Look out!"

"Go on! Go on!"

"H-harr!"
"*Kvas*! Rags!"
"Slap! Slap! Slap!"
. . . .
Market day!

25-31.7.1925

BREED MORE GOATS

As you are well aware, the population of Ukraine is a milk-demanding sucker. Hence it follows we need milk, milk and more milk. Everyone knows that if we don't give children milk, they turn to potatoes and salted cucumbers. And when you refuse them potatoes and everything else, the children die. And this, as you all know, is a detrimental thing...

Milk is obtained from cows. But now, because the drought has destroyed our harvests, the population has destroyed the cows. And as you all know, dead cows give no milk. Hence it follows we should turn to goats.

Goats have their advantages. They are only one third the size of cows and consume a sixth of the food. And yet cows and goats produce the same quantity of milk, since goat's milk is eight times as nutritious as cow's milk. So, if any of you aren't used to goat's milk, follow the example of the city's thrifty stallholders – add seven glasses of water to each glass of goat's milk, and you have real cow's milk.

Apart from milk, goats give wool. One goat can give up to a pound of wool each year. Well, in a hundred years you'll have close on a hundred-weight of wool. Now that's capital for you. *Foreign Trade* pays a high price for wool, so they can exchange it abroad for combs, document wallets, shoe polish and agricultural machinery.

Milking goats in winter, spring and autumn presents no great problems. The goat is tethered, the housewife sits on a stool and methodically pulls on the organs called teats. These teats are located head-down in the space between the hind legs, on a wide base called the udder.

Goats have two teats. If, when you sit down to milk a goat, you notice a few more teats on the belly toward the front end, it means you're milking a sow. Get up then and yell: "Shoo-shoo!" The sow will move away, and you can then find the goat, tether it and milk it dry.

Milking in summer presents a few more difficulties. Anatomy shows that goats have a very short organ for driving away flies, notably the tail. So, in summer, to make the goat stand still, a member of the family (if you've a small family, you can hire someone especially for the purpose) has to drive the flies away with a burdock leaf. The goat stands still then and the milk splashes in squirts into a previously positioned bowl.

When choosing a goat, be careful not to buy a billygoat. Because billygoats can't be milked. In the past five years three billygoats at the Priputin Research Station gave on an average not a single drop of milk.

So, farmers, let's breed more goats!

January, 1922

SHEEP BREEDING

The term 'sheep breeding' means to raise sheep...

And sheep, as you know, are very useful animals, providing us with milk, wool, sheepskins, mutton and lambs; and lambs give us lambskins, roast lamb and shashlik...

Sheep are very useful and raising them is a profitable business for any household.

So, farmers, go ahead and raise sheep...

They're easy to graze and not difficult to shear, and in winter they're no trouble to feed, for sheep will eat the coarsest hay, and sheep will grind down both weeds and straw...

There isn't much trouble with wool either. Just clip, wash, comb, spin and weave it... That's all there is to it...

And with mutton and roast lamb, it's also a breeze, no effort at all, just sink your teeth into it...

So sheep breeding doesn't appear to be that difficult or taxing...

There is one drawback to breeding sheep, though, which so exasperates shepherds that they scream:

"Slay me, or I'll die! By God, I'll lie down right here and die!"

The drawback is the ram.

He is only needed for two or three days each year to service your dozen or so sheep, yet you need to keep him all year long!

If you don't, there won't be any lambs...

And if you do, you have to feed the devil all year long...

The act of feeding him is nothing, but you have to ensure that he doesn't inseminate other people's sheep for nothing.

Now that's the hitch!

You keep a ram, and fifty farmers around you don't, relying on yours... You can go to them:

"Good-day!"

"Good-day!"

"My ram's in with the flock... We'll have to work this one out fairly... You'll have lambs too, but I have to feed him! Thirty copecks for each of your sheep, and he can go for his life..."

"Ah, why the thirty copecks?"

"What do you mean, *why*? So you'll have lambs!"

"But they'll appear anyway."

"I'll have you know there won't be any lambs!"

"Ah..."

Here is where it all begins...

"Sew the ram an apron, woman."

"They won't pay? Lousy people..."

An apron is made for the ram...

The ram ventures into the common flock in the morning, looking like a neat housemaid with his apron...

You won't have any damned lambs this year!

The ram returns home.

Breathing heavily, brow dripping, horns awry, apron hanging to one side, dragging his feet...

Grinning contentedly.

. . . .

"Tie him up and don't let him out! Keep him in the stall!"

The ram is tied up to the manger...

"Go and give the ram some hay!"

At that moment, a sheep bleats in the field.

The ram does a high jump. First prize! The manger scoots about the stall like a car.

The farmer's wife enters with the hay and he goes for her:

"Whack!"

The woman somersaults out of the stall, followed by the hay, which is followed by the ram, which is followed by the manger.

"Untie him, or he'll kill himself!"

One chop with the axe and the ram takes off like a prize racehorse, bounding over fences, sailing across gardens on his way to the field.

"Ba-a-ah!"

. . . .

Slay me or I'll die! By God, I'll die!

That's the hardest part of breeding sheep – keeping a ram and stopping it from reaching other people's sheep.

The rest is smooth sailing.

5-6.08.1925

SNIPE

For snipe hunters, the dog is the main thing!

I don't expect you to understand such an assertion straight away.

It's clear that a snipe isn't a dog, but a bird, yet every hunter knows that hunting snipe without a dog is tantamount to celebrating a wedding without music.

So if you want to discuss snipe, you must first discuss dogs, for without a setting dog you won't even see a snipe, let alone eat one.

But first, the... snipe.

Snipe are small marsh birds, grey with white feathers on their belly, very swift, with a very long bill and long legs; they break cover with a characteristic cry and fly off in crazy zig-zags, as if they've had a good stiff drink before taking off.

When roasted, snipe is scrumptious!

A delicacy!

Keep in mind that snipe is one of those few game birds which are roasted whole, guts and all; just stick the bill under one wing, baste them with some butter – and into the oven.

God forbid there's some cream about and a glass of you know what – I tell you, it's such a symphony then, that... let's set off for snipe right away...

I'll repeat it again: snipe without a dog is neither a delicacy nor a symphony, for without a dog there will be no snipe.

So, let's talk about the dog!

What a dog is, you all know: a head, four legs, a tail, and it barks.

We'll look at hunting dogs a little more closely, and seeing as we're talking about snipe, we are interested in setting dogs.

These come in several breeds:

a) Retrievers.

b) Gordon Setters.

c) Irish Setters.

d) Pointers.

e) Continental Setters.

f) Griffons.

g) Spaniels.

h) Poodles. These days the breed has degenerated into pampered lap dogs.

Which breed is the best?

The one you go hunting with.

When you get yourself a retriever, for instance, then no one in the world ever had a retriever like yours.

"What a dog! A real Edison! It's a fact! Listen, one day we were out hunting..."

And so it goes on...

Whether you listen or not, there really never was a dog like this one.

So, what breed do I suggest you get?

The breed you've already got or have your eye on.

A novice hunter, unbound by family hunting tradition, begins searching for a dog after buying his first rifle.

His mother-in-law, always a beautiful old woman, hearing of her dear son-in-law's desire to obtain a dog, says to him in a tender, affable voice (as mothers-in-law inevitably do), stressing the sibilant consonants:

"You need a s-s-setter! Akulina Kuzminish-sh-shna has a s-s-splendid dog! Loves s-s-setting! And more importantly, it's-s-s hous-s-se trained! I'll as-s-sk Akulina Kuzminish-sh-shna! Sh-sh-she'll be having pups-s-s s-s-soon! If by s-s-some s-s-stroke of good luck they don't all die! Very pure-bred pups-s-s!"

A month or two later you receive your splendid setter.

You're overjoyed: it's the first hunting dog you've ever had. It's yours! All yours!

You stroke it, and cuddle it, looking after it as if it was your own son, the dearest thing in the world.

You buy it a collar and a leash, and a while later take it with you to the hunting lodge, to the dog section, for an expert opinion.

You show it to a stern-looking fellow and look at him the way you once looked at your father, when, stern and preoccupied, he glanced at you tenderly and patted you on the head.

"Well?" you ask. "What do you think of my doggy? Isn't he nice and pure-bred? Ha?!"

The stern fellow gives the dog a long searching stare, and then looks across at you and says indifferently:

"It's a mongrel!"

"But I was assured it was a setter!"

"Then it's a mongrel-setter!" the fellow retorts.

"What do I do now?" you ask anxiously.

"Do now? It's not even worth attaching it to this leash, the leash is much too good. Just tie a bit of string round its neck. Neither its papa nor its mama has ever slept even near anything pure-bred! It's a complete mongrel!"

After this you engage your mother-in-law in short, curt dialogue, after which your mother-in-law sums up:

"Akulina Kuzminishna isn't like that! And I never dreamt that my Liuda (Liuda, of course, being your wife) could ever have made such a mistake about her life-long partner, and she's all I have, and where will I go now, and who'll there be to make her, and not only her, such nice doughnuts now? Young people have become so ungrateful. When a mother recommends a dog, you should remember after all, that the dog was recommended by your mother! Because I'm not only Liuda's mum, I'm your mother now as well. It's impossible, therefore, that the dog's a mongrel, rather than a setter! I can smell a mongrel! Liuda, let me smell it!"

A novice hunter's first dog is always a difficult dog.

It will be easier later on...

Later, after you have made friends with hunters and their dogs, after you have heard about the world-famous black pointer Cambise, and the famous retriever Ali, and the celebrated gordon Joe, then you'll get yourself a dog more to your liking.

If you prefer pointers, you'll be told:

"Vasyl Ivanovych has a pointer bitch with Cambise blood in her. Even Cambise himself once jumped over her, when she was getting out of the train with her owner at Boryspil Station!"

You become the owner, for argument's sake, of a beautiful pointer pup...

What should you call it?

Unequivocally, it must be Jack, or Joe, or Stack!

Never in your life call it Brovko, or Tsyatsya (if it's a bitch), or Tern, God help you: such a name can wreck a dog's talents for life, even though it may be a veritable god.

So you walk, or carry, or drive the pup home.

"Great dog, eh?" you ask everyone at home.

Screwing up her eyes, your mother-in-law peers at you and the dog, and retires to her room without uttering a word.

Your wife Liuda glances first at her mother, who is at the same time your mother-in-law, pats the dog on the head and says:

"It's a nice little dog! Will it have distemper soon?"

"I suppose so," you reply.

"The sooner, the better! They say that after a dog's had distemper, it won't die."

"Yes, it doesn't die much then!"

"Can it die from distemper?"

"My oath!"

"If only the distemper would come sooner!"

"Where can we make a place for him?" you ask nicely.

And you hear your mother-in-law's suggestion from the adjoining room, with a heavy emphasis on the sibilant consonants and the vowels:

"Perhaps you could buy it a double-bed? Or a separate couch?"

"Mamma," your wife placates her, "why are you getting upset?! It'll have distemper soon!"

The training of your hunting dog begins. Everything depends on how well trained it is: the success of your hunt, and the beauty and pleasure you experience when hunting with a pure-bred dog.

The day after the likeable pure-bred pup has settled into your apartment, the talk begins:

"Who's going to clean up after him?"

"Not me!" retorts your mother-in-law.

"I've cleaned up after it five times today," your wife announces, "and it still hasn't got distemper!"

"I'll clean up!" you announce decisively. "Where have all our rags gone? There were rags everywhere before, and now there's not one to be seen anywhere!"

So, you clean up after it...

It's rather late, you've cleaned up after Jack, placed him in his basket and retired to bed.

Jack misses his mother, and his brothers and sisters. Jack begins to whimper ever so pitifully.

Your mother-in-law shuffles out and benevolently placates Jack:

"Shut up! Shut up, you stupid mutt! Cark it, why don't you!"

At this moment, you clear your throat and call out:

"Jack, baby! Go to sleep, puppy!"

And your mother-in-law follows this with:

"Sleep puppy! Sleep baby! Fall into an eternal sleep, nice little doggy."

Jack's fallen asleep, your mother-in-law's fallen asleep, and you drift off too...

And as you do so, you hear your wife pleading in her sleep:

"Distemper! Distemper! Come on, distemper! Hurry up and come!"

And so, your beloved pure-bred Jack begins his life in your home.

He grows up, you wipe up after him.

You wipe the floor and take Jack for walks.

If you don't want to wipe up after him too often, then you have to take him for walks often, and if you don't take him for walks often, then you have to wipe up after him often.

To take a teeny pure-bred pup for a walk from the fifth or sixth floor five or six times a day is a very pleasant sporting pastime.

Right away you begin to teach Jack various necessary hunting skills: to heel, to fetch, or to seek out some hidden object, etc.

It is especially rewarding to teach the dog to find your slippers.

A pure-bred dog will master this skill in two to three days, and a fortnight later it'll be fetching the slippers of your whole family and all the neighbours who live in the same communal flat.

Joyous times set in when your dog begins to teethe.

One fine morning you wake up to the loud whimpering of your little pup and the loud screaming of your wife Liuda:

"My best ones! Oh, God! My only decent pair of shoes!"

"What's the matter?" you ask.

"He's eaten my best shoes!"

"Who's eaten your best shoes?"

"Your Jack!"

For the next fortnight, your wife addresses you very formally...

And a while later, all relations whatsoever are severed between you and your respected mother-in-law, after her beloved slippers are completely demolished.

Nevertheless, you continue to love Jack, he can already fetch sticks, he looks for objects, and you were witness yourself in the courtyard to his first setting of the neighbour's speckled hen.

Before you had time to tell him to strike, he had the hen's whole tail in his mouth, and the hen was squawking desperately from the shed roof.

Other incidents occur: you come home from work and even your loving son, Yurko, won't talk to you.

"What's the matter?" you inquire.

Silence. Tense silence. All you can hear is the whole family breathing heavily.

"Yura, dearest, what happened?"

"Jack gobbled up ten rissoles."

And if a similar situation occurs just before Christmas, then you'll hear:

"All that's left of the turkey is the parson's nose!"

"He must have begun on its neck!" you say. I mean, what else can you say?

And so it continues until the first anniversary of your dog's birth. After that it's not a bad idea to place the dog in the care of an expert trainer, who'll make your dog into one of a kind.

But that's up to you.

All I can say is that while your dog is with the trainer you will go about in an old suit and old shoes, and your wife will never wear a pair of fashionable shoes.

And you'll know the price of oatmeal and millet, and be well aware of the fact that your Jack devours a minimum of four horses every month. But finally, Jack is ready for your first independent snipe hunt.

"Point!"

"Go!"

Jack dashes forward and from under him jumps... an enormous toad.

Returning from the hunt, you tell your mates: "I sent Jack off to see if there were any snipe on the marsh. Jack raced off, rushing this way and that way, sniffing everything in sight, and returned with his tongue hanging out.

"'What,' I asked him, 'no snipe?'

"'None!' he replied."

* * *

Snipe, my friends, must be roasted whole, guts and all.

Ah, what tasty, noble, tender game!

October, 1945

HOW TO COOK
AND EAT WILD DUCK SOUP

The French have a saying: 'To have rabbit stew, you need to have a rabbit'...

If we translate the saying into Ukrainian, we'll get: 'To have wild duck soup, you need to have a wild duck'...

There once lived a famous ornithologist called Mensbeer, who on the basis of many years of observations and scientific research came to the conclusion that apart from frequenting markets, wild ducks could also be found in meadow lakes, in reeds, on calm stretches of water, and on the cradle rivers of our emerald Soviet Fatherland...

...In short, you set off for the meadow lakes, the reeds, and the calm stretches of water...

It goes without saying that you take a rifle along with you (this is a thing which shoots), some shells and various other hunting paraphenalia, without which one can't aim properly and hit the first time, without missing. This includes: a knapsack, a loaf of bread, some tinned food, cucumbers, tomatoes, a dozen hard-boiled eggs and a small tumbler... The tumbler is for bailing out the boat when it leaks...

You set out with a group of five or so friends, because wild ducks love to go into saucepans as a result of collective effort...

In the train carriage (or on the back of a truck) you'll always hear:

"Hell! I forgot my tumbler! D'you bring yours?"

"Yes!"

"Well, when we're together, you'll have to lend me yours! And if I'm on my own I'll have to make do from the 'neck'!"

In hunting terminology, the 'neck' is the name for that part of a hunter's boat called 'starboard' on ocean-going vessels.

Wild ducks love to be killed on serene evenings, when the sun has already slipped from the evening stage and has fallen below the blood-crimson horizon, sending you its last golden greeting before going to sleep... This is in the evening... And in the morning, wild ducks break cover very early to seek your gunshots, at the very crack of dawn.

Hunters call these times 'watches' – the evening and morning 'watch'...

At these times, you hear a noise above you, and before you, and behind you, and to your right, and to your left – the whistle of duck wings.

You go 'bang!' here, and 'bang!' there, and 'bang!' over there.

Ah, unforgettable moments!

You're late for the evening watch. This is a must... Being late for the evening watch is a hunting rule. Even before you leave home you know that you certainly won't make the evening watch, and because of this you make everything ready on the morning of your departure, forgetting something even then, and when it's time to go, you rush out of the apartment and fly off to the station, or your car. When acquaintances ask you where you're going, you retort: 'I'm hurrying to be late for the evening watch.' And you gallop off.

In short, you're late... You reach the lake only after the ducks have 'turned off their motors', brushed their teeth, done their evening exercises, and are asleep with their heads resting on water lilies.

But you're not worried, for near every meadow lake there's always a stack or rick of very fragrant hay... You walk up to the haystack and make yourself comfortable... Spreading your coat out on the hay, you stretch out on your back and rest, surveying the deep blue-black starry sky... And resting, you muse...

While you're musing there to your heart's content, we're going to prepare for the morning watch...

"Well, how about it, friends, let's get everything ready in the evening, so we won't have to muck around in the morning, and can just grab our rifles and take up our positions. Where's the... tumbler?"

"I specifically asked her to pack it!"

"What, can't you find it?"

"No!"

"I've got mine! As a rule, I tie it to the inside of my knapsack when I get home, so that I won't forget it the next time. I think you fret over it more than if you had forgotten your rifle!"

"I'll have to start tying one to the inside of mine as well! But today you'll have to lend me yours... It's a capricious thing, I tell you, having it straight from the 'neck'... The air is clean, you take a few deep breaths, and before you've had time to even sigh in the dark, the level's fallen from around the 'neck' to the 'bottom'.

This is where the most interesting part of a duck hunt begins.

When your old, experienced hunting friends begin to recount various unusual incidents which have occurred to them in their hunting life.

Common to all hunting stories is the fact that they are all completely true, that everything really happened, that 'when I tell you, you won't believe me, but it's a fact!'

...Some cosmic youth hurls stars about the heavens, leaving golden streaks in the blue-black chasm, the Heavenly Cart creaks on its way, lowering its thill, the Milky Way slowly grows paler, and around the haystack a beautiful lace of hunting stories is being woven...

And the air is so easy to breathe...

Slowly the narrator's voice quiets, then suddenly breaks off and there's only silence...

Your neighbour sighs deeply...

"What are you thinking about there, Ivan Ivanovych?"

"America! What ingenious technology."

"What d'you mean?"

"They say they've developed a double-barrelled tumbler!"

Silence...

Everyone is asleep...

'Very early in the morn, and at the first crack of dawn' someone elbows you in the side:

"Get up! Get up! It's time!"

"H-h-h! M-m-m!"

"Get up!"

"M-m-m!"

"B-b-bang!"

Screaming 'air raid!', you jump to your feet and run!

"Where you headed?! Eh?!"

"The bomb shelter?"

"The heck on you! I've just shot at a mallard!"

"And you missed?"

"Well of course I missed! Who wouldn't have, when the devil spirited you off in search of a bomb shelter! I nearly ended up in the lake!"

The morning watch has begun...

Now everything depends on your skill, your mastery and practice...

A duck, as you know, is a bird. It flies...

How do you shoot it?

It's very simple: always aim for its eye. And then press the trigger.
Bang! – and bag it. Bang! – and bag it.

And when you've had no luck, that is when you go 'bang-bang!' and there's nothing to bag. But don't fret. Try to drive or walk home via a market, or on seeing another hunter who is carrying several ducks, quip:

"They must be several rubles apiece now..."

Because whatever you do, the ignorant members of your family will inspect your bag and ask you:

"Ducks must be expensive now, eh?"

Take no notice of the remark and set about making the amber wild duck soup straight away...

The first and most important thing is to pluck the duck. This is best done in your study. So the plucked feathers don't get in your way, open the door and windows, so there's a decent draft, and then pluck a handful of feathers, let the draft pick them up, and the feathers won't bother you... Then when the duck is plucked, your study is like a feather mattress...

After you've plucked it, trot off to your mother, or your wife, or your sister, whoever you've been blessed with:

"I've finished plucking it, mamma! Can you make some soup!"

Mothers usually come up with a very tasty result.

When your wife or your mother sighs and exclaims:

"This is no duck, it's a chicken!"

Declare with authority:

"This is a duck. Ducks have all become like this now. Stratified..."

"Why is its throat slit?"

"Why? Why? You're all so curious to know everything. It was flying along, saw me taking aim, realised its chips were down, and so it slit its throat. What's so strange about that?! Just go and boil it, please!"

So there's still the last stage of our exercise left – to eat the soup.

How do we eat it?

With a spoon!

Having eaten your fill, you can stretch out on the couch and read *Hunting Notes* by Ivan Sergeyevich Turgenev.

It's a marvellous book!

1945

CARP

I

A wonderful forest. Mixed. With enormous oaks and ashes and elms and pines. But mostly oaks and pines. On a still day, there's not a rustle in the forest: dead quiet, broken only by the occasional flute call of a golden oriole, the knocking of a woodpecker, the warble of a goldfinch... And then there's silence once more...

In a breeze, the oaks creak, their leaves flutter angrily, the pines rustle endlessly... There's a lake in the middle of the forest, embellished on one side with bulrushes...

Somehow it turned out that on one side pines gaze into the water, and on the opposite side – oaks... To the left of the lake is a dam, to the right stretch meadows with green shrubbery, willows and lush grass.

There are carp in the lake. Whoppers.

"The carp in this lake are ginormous. As big as bathtubs!"

And how one wants to catch one of these 'bathtubs'...

Especially after being told:

"What?! When you get a bite, when it yanks on the line, when it moves off – don't even think of striking it! Pray that it gets off the line itself. Otherwise you'll lose your hook, and line, and rod, and you'll end up in the water yourself, if you don't grab hold of a tree in time! That's our carp for you! Real thoroughbreds! They're a special breed – hybrids. A cross between 'mirror' and 'Simmental' carp."

Little wonder you want to catch a hybrid like that.

Carp is best taken at dawn. Especially when the sun's first soft rays cut through the oak treetops and gild the leaves, which tremble chastely, quaking ever so gently...

When the sun's rays gild the oak leaves, the sun bursts forth from the oak thickets and falls on the lake – then lake, bulrushes and sand are all golden.

The rays bounce off the water and fly to the far side of the lake, and then the pines and ashes and elms turn to gold. The rays continue on and out of sight... Leaving a joyous and playful wake...

And everything springs to life, everything rejoices.

When a carp jumps out of the golden water, it's golden as well...

The carp is like a bathtub... A golden bathtub...

See what the sun does with its joyous, playful rays...

Only don't think that the sun rises over the lake in the east... No!

It rises on your left, through the oaks, on purpose, so that it can gild the oaks first...

Oh, that cunning sun!

It wants everything that its rays touch to sparkle, shine, rejoice and flourish...

Cunning, cunning sun!

II

But how do you catch the carp that lives in this lake in the wonderful mixed forest with such mighty oaks and such tall slender pines and sharp-leafed maples? How?

First, let's consider if it's worth one's while to catch the carp?

Of course it is!

Have you ever experienced the moment when a carp bites? Have you? If you haven't, then you simply must, and if you have – you'll itch to relive that moment once again!

Imagine you're sitting at the lake's edge early in the morning. Dawn is breaking. The sky bursts into flame on your left... That's the sun rising... You have a rod in hand. Your line is strong, your hook is of hardened steel. You've baited the hook with potato, cooked just the way carp like it – not too soft and not too hard, just right. You eye the float, like you've never even eyed your sweetheart... So intently, with such desire, such longing. And suddenly, the float goes – bob! Your heart goes – thump! Another bob! Another thump! And your float quickly swims off and disappears into the water. When the float begins to quickly swim off, something cold from under your heart begins to roll down, down, down, past your appendix, lower, lower, lower, until you feel the ball of cold hit the soles of your feet and they grow cold. You grab hold of the rod, and strike! And you feel something quivering in your hands! Your line is taught as a bow, and the rod is curved! Yes, it's a carp! You reel it into shore... The line zig-zags across the water and the rod jerks this way and that... The carp is close to shore now. Its head appears out of the water, you can see its back. It is trying to break free, thrashing about, twisting into a doughnut... But you don't slacken the line, you reel it in... Another step, and it'll be landed. Your heart is churning away, you're breathing heavily and quickly. You can already imagine it stuffed, or marinated, or simply fried, and a great steaming soup being made from its head... Suddenly – splash! You go – yank! – and the hook is bare. Stunned for a moment, the carp lies before you... What moments...!

Anyway, on this occasion there is no carp: it got away.

What do you do?

There have been cases where the fisherman has jumped into the water to grab the carp with his hands. Splash! Fully clothed, in boots, together with his bag of potatoes, his cigarettes and a pass to the resort town of Hahry in his pocket... Alas, in vain! Carp don't go for passes to Hahry, not even for potatoes in a bag. Only when the potato is on a hook.

More restrained fishermen blurt something out at such times, the exact words depending on their temperament, and bait the hook with fresh potato. They cast their lines again and snort angrily.

When a neighbour asks:

"Big one got away?"

"Enormous fellow, almost black!" they reply and continue to snort.

Of course, worse can happen if you get a giant carp on your line: then there's only a teeny piece of your line left and your hook graces its upper lip...

In such cases, when a neighbour asks what happened, one replies sternly:

"It tore the line to shreds!"

Among other things, it is not recommended to leave your rod on shore unsecured and to go for a walk in the forest, because it is not infrequent for shepherds to be heard hollering:

"Hey, mate! Your rod's swum off! Sped off like a motor boat!"

Then you have to undress and chase about the lake after your rod...

In such instances, the carp is a master of ridicule – soon as you get near your rod, it gives a tug and swims off... Further and further away!

So tell me then, please, is it worth fishing for carp or not, when you have to suffer such trying moments?

We're not talking here of the bliss one experiences when the carp is landed and brought home, and marinated, or stuffed, or simply fried!

And you snack on it and boast to everyone:

"Boy, did it grab hold of the line! Boy, did it speed off! But I'm not one to let go…"

. . . .

"Well, eat your fill!"

26.7.1951

HOW I WENT FISHING

It's morning. And what a lyrical morning!

Sky above, earth below. And a lake before me...

Know what a lake is?

It's an extremely large deep bowl in the ground filled with water, rather than "Supe a la peisanne" (as they wrote in the "Renaissance").

And in that water there are fish and crayfish...

My aim as a fisherman is to catch the fish and any crayfish that happen along.

That's for one.

Secondly, to get enjoyment from all of this, to relax, and to make soup from my fresh catch...

For this reason, I've taken the following with me:

a) Obligatory Decree No. 118 of the Kharkiv Gubernial Executive Committee (rules on how to fish),

b) a ruler,

c) a pair of dividers,

d) an umbrella (for shade!),

e) a basket holding half a dozen salted roaches[23], a bottle of pepper vodka (of pre-war quality), two pounds of bread and other things,

f) my identity card,

g) a membership card,

h) a fishing-rod,

i) my wife.

Everything then as prescribed...

I've cast my rods...

"Biting, uncle?"

"Get outa here! They'll bite in due course!"

---

23   In this case, roach is not an insect. It's a fish (Rutilus rutilus caspicus), a member of the carp family that lives in fresh and brackish water in Europe. Typical of some Eastern European foods, the fish is salted and sun-dried.

The fellow keeps walking and his voice carries across the water:
"Fishing, he is fishing,
For a dinner of salted roach."
"Go ahead, laugh…"

For the first two and a half hours I looked stoically at the water and thought: 'Just look: hydrogen and oxygen, any old H_2O, and yet it holds so many fish.'

And I, you could say, am a man, a *Homo Sapiens*, but not even the mangy sprats are biting!

Suddenly the float went: bob-bob-bob!

Tug!

"Got him! Aha! Catch him, woman, catch him! Hold on there! Caught him?"

"Yes!"

"A crucian carp? Let's have the ruler and the dividers! Have a gander at the fishing rules. What does it say there? 'Crucian carp no shorter than five inches. Measure from the centre of the eye to the anal fin…' Good! Find the eye!"

"Found it!"

"Find the centre of the eye. Found it? Lay the ruler to it. Ye-e-es! Hold it there. Look for the anal fin now."

"I have no idea where it is."

"Look at the back! If it's anal, it means it's at the back. In the anus. Found it?"

"Hasn't got one!"

"Have you forgotten your zoology? What did they teach you in those high schools? Here, give it to me."

"Oh, that's it!"

"What's *it*?"

"The fish jumped into the water!"

"Really! And you attended evening lectures! And worked for the Co-op Union! Can't you even hold onto a mangy fish?"

Bob-bob-bob! The float again.

"'Other fish'? How much do they allow for 'other fish'?"

"*Five inches.*"

"Gimme the ruler. Found the eye. Turn over, you 'other fish'. Where's your anal fin? Hasn't got one. Look, there's no fin! A pike must have bitten it off! What now?"

"I haven't the slightest idea."

"I'll throw it back in. Back into the lake, you! I don't know, swimming about without anal fins! And then we have to answer for it!"

"Oh, oh, oh! A crayfish! Come quickly! Take a look what it says about crays? How do you measure them?"

"Three and a half inches. From the tip of the head to the tip of its tail."

"Gimme the ruler! We'll start from the head..."

"You've got the tail there!"

"What d'you mean? This is the tail! The head's on its neck!"

"That's its tail, stupid! You don't know anything yourself, and you go abusing everyone else!"

"What's the difference where I start measuring from?"

"Well then?"

"Three and a quarter inches! Go to hell! Piss off, you! Couldn't grow a lousy quarter of an inch longer, could you? And you come crawling out of the water!"

"Off you go back home."

We had salted roach for dinner.

30.5.1923

TRIED IT?

Ivan Stepanovych did not believe in vets.

Wasn't it all the same, a backyard crutcher[24] or a vet? Sure it was...

"Would I take my colt to a vet? Never in the world. A backyard crutcher will do him, he's no gentleman... He'll tie them up tightly and yank them off. Just like cracking a nut."

He said this and went to bed... Fell fast asleep and had a dream. A crutcher with a piece of rope came up to him... He made a noose and tightened it around Ivan's nose, made a loop below his knee, and pulled his nose toward his knee, hitting him behind the knee. Ivan Stepanovych crashed to the ground with a croak. And then the crutcher took a pair of pincers and grabbed Ivan Stepanovych between the legs like a mad dog. Then he got a knife, dirty and rusty... A quick slice with the knife! Cut them off and dressed the wound with some dirty twine...

Ivan Stepanovych lay moaning... in excruciating pain... They brought him home... A week passed and his wound would not heal... Puss oozed from it... He seemed to have a fever... Two weeks passed and still the wound had not healed... Ivan Stepanovych grew thin and pale, his soul was ready to leave his body... He ached all over and his strength was ebbing... The wound was raw and became infested with maggots...

"Oh! Oh! Oh!" groaned Ivan Stepanovych...

"Why are you groaning and thrashing your legs about?"

Ivan Stepanovych blinked and saw his wife beside him.

"Why are you groaning?"

"The crutcher fixed me. The wound won't heal..."

"Will you come to your senses? Holy Mother of God! What's wrong with you?"

"Oh, the crutcher!"

"What crutcher? Wake up!"

Ivan Stepanovych sat up and looked around.

---

24   Colloquial Australian term for a person who crudely desexes male animals with a knife.

"Phew! What a dream! My God!"
Now Ivan Stepanovych takes his livestock to the vet.

1925

THE SEXUAL PROBLEM

What's happened to our Kharkiv? I just can't make it out!

Stroll down any street and from every fence, every billboard, posters announce: The Sexual Problem, Secrets of Love, Sexual Hygiene, The Light and the Shade of the Sexual Problem, Marital Hygiene.

Lecturers from Moscow, Leningrad and our locals, professors, doctors of medicine and ordinary lecturers of renown have so fascinated Kharkiv with the 'sexual problem', that you can't help noticing it…

It's as if they expect you to drop everything and sit down to watch the sexual problem, to seek 'the light and the shade' of it.

Almost every day, in the drama hall, the library, the Missouri Theatre.

Is it such a burning and acute issue, that every citizen must attend?

Agreed, there is a 'sexual problem', there are all kinds of rules associated with it, but have mercy on my soul – why take things so far?

Not one of those lecturers comes to speak on the sowing campaign, for instance…

Not interesting?

You can tie the two in… Choose a subject like 'The Sexual Problem and its Effect on the Sowing Campaign'.

Useful and interesting.

Though a peasant, Dmytro Fedorovych, once told me: 'When you've swung a scythe from four in the morning till nine at night, you sleep so soundly, that there's no sexual problem whatsoever.'

So I thought that if we were to make the lecturers and their audiences put in a few days solid work running behind grain broadcasters or helping collect hay bales in the fields, or hammering away for eight hours in a boiler repair plant, we shouldn't have any problems at all.

04.04.1924

'DOWN WITH SHAME'

On the path of our grey humdrum working life, on the boundless plains of untouched work, amid work which has inundated us from all sides in gigantic waves, fate has sent us a sumptuous flower, borne of impetuous human minds...

That lovely sumptuous flower is called the 'Down with Shame' society.

Across the cities of the expansive USSR naked people are emerging into the streets, their 'shame' covered with a mere fig leaf, and they ramble through the streets to the delight of the workers, peasants and Soviet public servants, but especially to the delight of the children and homeless urchins...

What a splendid sight to behold!

Graceful as gazelles, handsome as the Belvedere Apollo, attractive as the Venus of Milos, they carve up the dull mist of our existence with the white rays of their bodies...

What a splendid idea!

And how unsplendid the police are!

They go and arrest them...

Why, if we may ask them? (the police, of course)

Why do the police enjoy privileges in these matters?

Why are the police able to take these splendid young people away to the regional police station so that they can admire them there, while we mortals are denied this privilege?

It's simply unjust...

This matter needs to be set out, so that everyone can enjoy it.

* * *

What a splendid idea!

I can already imagine that blessed time when this takes off...

When the 'Down with Shame' society becomes legalized and registered with the Central Cooperative Committee!

You're on your way to work...

And in front of you, behind you, and on either side gambol graceful naked bodies…

The head accountant of the Wormseed Trust is rushing along with his thirty-five years of service. He has a solid fig leaf, large and thoroughly ironed, as befits a man of good standing on a special allowance…

And here comes the young secretary from the All-Ukrainian Central Executive Committee, with her tiny narrow fig leaf with a little bow, and there near her navel there's a small mole… She's flirting… Her leaf rises and falls… All joy, all sparkle…

Meanwhile Fedora Sylivna is floating down Seminary Descent on her way to market. She sells butter. There's no fig leaf big enough for her needs. So she has a large combination leaf: half of it is burdock, the other half – cabbage… But even this combination isn't enough… So she gracefully covers the rest with a frypan…

Here's a reporter rolling down Libknecht Street. He's hurrying to an interview and has forgotten his fig leaf… So he covers himself with his briefcase…

"How about not swinging your briefcase about so energetically, comrade!"

. . . .

Such a splendid idea!

Except in winter when the footpaths freeze over they'll need to spread sand on them…

Otherwise, if you happen to slip at the top of University Hill and fly headlong down the stairs, then you'll really get rid of your 'shame'.

Graze it clean off!

03.10.1924

GYNAECOLOGY

There's not much medical personnel in the rural areas...

It's the same here... A sizeable village, surrounded on all sides by settlements, and the hospital's eight kilometres away.

However, praise to the Almighty, sanitary illiteracy is being slowly eradicated among the populace...

There's many an 'expert' here to cure all kinds of illnesses, beginning with 'the evil eye' and ending with 'rabies', but in no other branch are the Orthodox people as expert as in gynaecology, a very delicate science very much in demand in villages...

We won't be wrong in saying that just about every individual of the female sex knows at least something of what goes on when a stork circles above a house to bring the lucky one a boy or a girl...

And there are quite a good few specialist-gynaecologists with extensive practical experience, who earn eggs by the bushel and linen by the roll, deciding gynaecological matters much more swiftly and decisively than the eminent Professor Khazhynsky from Kharkiv...

One, two, and there you go!

There are no clinics or surgical theatres yet – the operations are carried out in a house, a store-room or a barn. Most of the experts are women, though there are a few male gynaecologists too.

There are even run-of-the-mill deacons, I've been told, who can perform an operation as easily as one-two-three.

———·———

I wanted to acquaint city folk with country practices in this field... For you often see a beautiful woman behind an office desk or an Underwood typewriter, or just walking down the street, and suddenly she becomes pensive and sad, her eyes turn misty and shadows fall on her lovely face...

I don't know, maybe it's only 'cause she wants to get married, but more often than not her mood is due to you know what...

Now here's what experienced daughters of the countryside do in such cases...

When Eve's descendant gets up in the morning and feels strange, having a craving for salted cucumbers, she starts jumping on the spot... Stands there, then crouches down and suddenly springs up wildly.

Thud! Thud!

And then she listens...

Nothing...

She shakes her head sadly and goes to weed the potatoes.

The next day, when her craving for salted cucumbers has become stronger and more persistent, she begins lifting heavy trunks.

Crouches down beside the trunk, embraces it with both arms and lifts it...

"What are you doing, Melasia?" her mother asks.

"Our trunk seems to be standing a little unevenly, so I decided to straighten it..."

"Let me give you a hand."

"No, it's all right... It's not that heavy... Look... Ho! Ho!"

"Are you crazy, you'll get a hernia!"

"Rubbish..."

After dragging the trunk about, the woman or girl stops and listens.

Nothing...

Then she goes behind the shed and squirms about there for a long time...

Father comes home and asks:

"Who the devil's tipped over our winnower?"

...The winnower is no help either...

There are numerous ways of doing such 'exercises with weights'...

Often you see a young girl bounding down to the river with a tub full of wet washing...

Or moving a cow in the stall from one corner to another...

But it's impossible to list all of them here...

And after each attempt she stands sadly and listens...

Nothing...

After this her face grows even sadder, and her eyes dart about the room...

Then she tries 'quinisation'[25].

She does the 'quinisation' until her head feels like church bells are splitting her head apart.

That doesn't work either...

Then they try the so-called artillery method...

Pack themselves full of gunpowder.

Doesn't fire...

Then it's into the rye after ergot spurs.

They eat spoonfuls of those spurs...

No change...

Then they steal a dozen eggs from the pantry and go off to see an 'expert'.

"Darling."

Here the self-help gynaecology finishes. Now the work is placed in the hands of a specialist.

———•———

Experts...

Now here, of course, we can't provide any details: each expert resorts to her own methods...

Usually for their instrument they use a large hairpin bent into a hook at one end...

This operation is called 'scratching out'...

Quite often a sharp spindle will serve the same purpose. This is called 'piercing'...

After the operation, the blood drips for eight kilometres to the nearest hospital.

And that's it.

After that, the woman goes about bent double for about six months...

"Something's wrong with me inside... Some call it 'the gnaws', others – 'colic'..."

The course of treatment is finished...

———•———

---

25   The use of quinine to treat malaria. Quinine, available over the counter, was used for self-induced abortion.

These methods can be easily adapted to city conditions, with a few small variations, of course.

Instead of a tub of clothes, the girl could run up and down stairs with a heavy Underwood typewriter. Or instead of a trunk, she could use a desk or try to move a steel safe about, if she works in an accountant's office, or even a cupboard full of files will suffice...

I won't write anything about the city 'experts': there are enough of them about.

23.07.1925

BLUE BOG

(A literary caricature of Mykola Khvylovy's writing style)

CHAPTER ONE

Bog – how bland...

Sounds so vague: bog...

But now fever – that's vivid. Tossing and turning... Sweating... Convulsions... Eyes red, lips red, breasts red, but the tongue is white... (Tongue – language – nation – oppression – liberation)...

Liberation – nation...!

Eh, people!

Arise ye people, before the flies and mosquitoes finish you off!

Bog sounds bland... Let's call it –

– A swamp...

Swine... wine... grapes... Press... Juice... Blood... Revolution...

Rat-a-tat! Rat-a-tat!

...The dawn glowed red...

It dayed...

The day came and the day passed...

...The day passed (to pass, to piss, toilet, the Terminological Commission of Hetman Skoropadsky's Ministry of Transport).

This is just waffle.

But now...

Under a dusky sky the black earth is pimpled with the buildings of a large city; the sun pierces the roads with flaming spears.

But more about the city later.

Now I am talking about buildings...

Buildings...

Buildings – single-storeyed, two-storeyed, three-storeyed, four-storeyed, and 'storeyed' and 'storeyed'...

Buildings to the left, buildings to the right, and a slithering road between them...

Between them...
Eh, remember:

> *And between these two very steep mountains*
> *A lone star rises.*

...Doors from the street... Doors into every building...

And this building has four exits, entries... Apartment exit, four-roomed apartment (I'll get in first! – from the back way!)...

In the apartment where Khaya is, not where Karlo Ivanovych is, there's a bed. Under the bed stands a bedpan (empty – Karlo Ivanovych has already emptied it).

Chamber pot – commander-in-chief (imperialist butchery)...

Khaya is in bed...

Let's just assume:

There are bedbugs in the bed. Dark-pink bedbugs. (There are bedbugs like that, you know, full of blood, full of itch, when you sleep in the steppe, or perhaps on the hay in the barn, or perhaps not)...

Yes, Khaya is in bed...

Karlo Ivanovych is by the window.

Khaya is a woman...

Why a woman...?

Maybe because her hips are broader, maybe because of something else.

And Karlo Ivanovych is a man (the pants)...

"Honeypie!" (that's Karlo Ivanovych)... I can't... We are northern people, we are frigid people. I can't... I can't right now!"

"You must... You must now... You know, I mustn't suffer: I've got woman trouble..." (That's Khaya).

"Honeypie! I can't any more. We are northern people..."

"Ba-a-astard!"

She shrieks, splitting her long, neglected pantaloons in four... (that's Khaya).

A pity about the pantaloons (my remark).

Aha!

Yes, well, I forgot to mention one thing.

Khaya is responsible...

Karlo Ivanovych is responsible!

Khaya pisses.

Karlo Ivanovych empties the bedpan. They're both responsible...

[...]

CHAPTER 8

And that "oh-oh-oh!" echoed far and wide.

Throughout valleys and mountains.

Mountains...

Crimea...

So, Khaya and Karlo Ivanovych arrived in Crimea...

They rented a room...

Khaya sits on a bed...

There's a bedpan under the bed.

(See chapter one)...

But don't just look at chapter one, look outside as well...

Mountains... Blue, blue mountains...

You know: climbing up mountains...

You know: it's high atop a mountain, and it's low in the valley...

Where did the mountains spring from...

But that doesn't concern me...

If I wrote where mountains sprung from, geologists would be out of a job...

And geology is an interesting science... Right?

There are still very many other very interesting sciences...

About the earth, and the sky, and the sun, and the stars...

What's that science about stars called?

Astronomy...?

But there's also gastronomy. Such an insignificant extra letter, but how it changes everything...

One is spacious, mysterious, bottomless like the heavens...

And the other is – NEP, the New Economic Policy.

Pot-bellied, wide-jowled and snuffling away... Like a steam engine, when it is being siphoned...

Thus:

"Sss... Sss..."

And you stand on the railroad track – and look...

To see where the rails run off to...!

The rails run far-far away...

And on either side are villages, towns, forests, mountains, valleys, marshes, and bogs...

Oh, at last!

'Bog'...
See, I told you, you'd get to 'bog'...
And now you have...
Full stop...
No, sorry, it's not a full stop yet, it's a comma...
...to the bog, which before dawn is embraced for the last time by blue...
always blue...
There, you see:
'Blue Bog'...
Full stop...
That's it...
Finito.
Kaput.

1930

TOURISTS

"So, what do you do? What's your profession?"

"Actually, doctor, I don't work at all. I write. I just sit and write..."

"You sit and write? Yes, well, you see, when you don't work, and just sit around and write, it doesn't mean it's bad for your lungs, it's just that because of your so-called work, a part of them does not breathe properly. The excursion of your lungs, as we doctors put it, is not complete. You sit hunched up, always in the same position... Well, you can well imagine, parts of the lungs breathe properly, while other parts are constricted... And with time ... You sit around like that for a year and parts of your lungs forget how to function properly. They wrinkle up, various manifestations of stagnation set in... Like a plough which begins to rust because it's not being used... So, you'll need to exercise them properly... We're lucky here... We've got mountains... The best thing for such lungs is to go up and down the mountains... Then your rib cage expands, your lungs are filled to the brim with air, their smallest nooks and crannies are smoothed out, all your blood is oxidized... You grow more cheerful, more jolly, the flush returns to your cheeks, you will be rejuvinated... Off with you into the mountains! It'll do you a world of good!"

"Thanks, doctor!"

...Off into the mountains we go!!

"Where you off to in such high spirits?"

"Into the mountains! My lungs aren't breathing properly! Incomplete excursion! Stagnation... My blood isn't oxidizing... I need to rejuvenate my body... To cheer up... Become more jolly... More handsome... To hell with sitting at a desk! I'm going to take brisk walks, exercise, regain my strength...! Ah, the good life!"

"It's a steep climb..."

"Steep? Steep, for us tourists? Nothing's steep for us tourists. For us tourists it's all flat. Steep?! Adieu!"

———•———

And the mountain… it's a decent mountain!! A good old mountain! It's called 'The

Cat'! Cheerfully we set off up the cliff face along steep paths, with a merry song on our lips:

A mountain this side,
A mountain that side…
And between these two very steep mountains
A lone star rises.

And the voice carries, and carries, and carries… It fans out… Fans out up to a dozen yards…

Up we go! Up we go!

"Ph-e-ew!"

"H-ha… another… mountain… that side."

To hell with it, it's a high one!

"And another one this si-i-ide!"

Ph-e-ew!

Take a rest!

Look! We tourists still have a long way to go!

…Come on, livelier there! All your lungs will be exercised! Your blood will be oxidized…!

Hurry, up you go!

. . . .

Oh! Is it still far to go?

Another rest!

Ph-e-ew!

Come on, get up, you tourist!

O-o-oh!

U-u-up we go! The mountain top's still miles away!

Another rest!

. . . .

C'mon, up you get!

Another rest!

. . . .

C'mon…

Another rest...

. . . .

And another...

. . . .

And another...

. . . .

One more...

. . . .

I've had it...

. . . .

"Anyone down there? Any God-fearing soul about? Catch me, intercept us tourists, 'cause my damned feet won't cling to the mountain any longer... Oh!"

...Send me at least our native elderberry in my path, oh Lord, if there's no Lebanese cedar – send me anything to grab hold of, or else they won't be able to piece me together...

...Caught hold of a pine!

Oh!

. . . .

I lay on a Tatar bed, stretched out like Jesus Christ, my calves feeling as if they'd had nails driven through them.

———•———

You expand your lungs, and twist your ankles... Stretch your legs and damage your lungs...

. . . .

Tourists, in short!

27.05.1924

CRIMEAN NIGHTS

[...]

Ah, those nights! Ah, those Crimean nights! Who dreamt them up? And why are they so blue, so clear? Why are they so intoxicating?

Ah, those nights! Ah, those Crimean nights!

Just look what they are doing to the people!

. . . .

"Hey, girls! Lonely there tonight?"

"Get lost, lamebrains!"

... And five minutes later, just five minutes of this magical Crimean night, and the girl's head is resting against the lamebrain's chest...

Soft voices... Hamstrings trembling... Heart thumping... Blood boiling...

Ah, those nights! Ah, those Crimean nights!

. . . .

And what sounds you emit, Crimean nights! What fragrances! What stealthy rustling! And those songs of yours! Those magical southern songs!

> *Eh, that rosy red apple,*
> *Colour deep pink!*
> *He loves her dearly,*
> *She couldn't care less!*

'She' doesn't love him! But no matter! She'll come 'round to loving him, for already from a nearby bush or another cliff the blueness of evening is disturbed by the words:

> *Oh, why was the night*
> *So beautiful then?...*

What songs! What marvellous southern songs! Such cypress-laden songs!

Bushes rustle! Bushes whisper! And in the bushes, spermatozoa snuggle up to chlamydia bacteria.

"What will happen? What can happen?"

And on Chatyr-Dag peak the demon shakes his hairy wings...

Intoxicated voices carry from the bushes:

"Ah, those sweet songs...!"
And the demon roars with laughter:
> *Those sweet songs?*
> *Maybe nothing will come of it...*
> *But maybe... Maybe there'll be kids...*
Oh, those nights! Ah, those Crimean nights!

. . . .

The Crimean night grows quiet. It grows dark and quiet...
And it breathes easily...
It breathes in the fresh Crimean air...
And the sea quietly laps at the shore...
The laurel trees are silent... The cypresses are silent.
The night is asleep...
Black shadows ensnare the windows... Silence fills the windows...
Silence... silence...
[...]

. . . .

Ah, those nights! Ah, those Crimean nights!

. . . .

Time to sleep!!!

29.05.1924

CRIMEAN MOON

(Another Lyrical Piece)

A golden Crimean moon!

Rising from the sea, from Istanbul itself…

With flashes of gold, rays of silk, magical and titillating, the Crimean moon bathes in the blue of the sea…

When the intoxicating night cloaks the Crimean shores with its blue-black wing, the Crimean moon appears, gilding that blue-black wing, scattering handfuls of gold upon the rocky shores, laughing, plunging golden daggers into the emerald waves…

The magnolia trembles in its golden cobwebs, and the Lebanese cedar bathes its needles in them too…

The cypress strains upward with all of its being, calling out like Sulamif to King Solomon:

"Look at me, moon!"

Black handsome cypress!

. . . .

What a charmer the Crimean moon is!

What a madcap!

How well it knows the workings of a person's soul, sidling up to it, echanting it, pleasing it, and then, having done its magical work, it laughs with a light golden laugh, rippling mirthfully upon the sea…

And people overburdened with worries, political, Soviet and professional, look at the moon and wave it aside:

"Get out of here!"

But the moon is a flatterer, it will wrap you in its silk, splash a handful of silver onto the sand, smile and point to a rose, or wink in the direction of a steep cliff, shine upon some ivy, expose a silvery poplar, and then pause in the heavens, waiting…

And then the person burdened with political, Soviet and professional worries straightens up and wanders off somewhere, badly wanting something, humming a tune, tapping with their right political-Soviet-professional foot, smiling...

"Ah, you madcap!"

. . . .

And then political, Soviet and professional people gaze up at the moon and sigh:

"Oh!"

And they set up moon committees with sections, sub-sections and departments...

And they wait for the moon. Meanwhile the wizard pairs them off and sends them flying into the bushes, onto the cliffs and into the sea...

'Moonlight bathing!'

Ah, those moonlit dips! They have such a strong influence on people's constitutions...

And the local post-office as well...

Women send telegrams from the Crimea to all corners of the Soviet Union:

'Love you! Kisses! Urgently require money!'

And from all corners of the Soviet Union telegrams rustle back to men in Crimea:

'Why aren't you writing? Up to your old tricks? Thrice-damned Ukrainian topknot!'

Ah, moon! Ah, you madcap!

. . . .

Nothing can overpower that moon! No one can put it in its place!

It's a magician!

Its power is invincible...

Were you to convene the most serious of committees here by the sea, any old Commissariat or the board of Ukrainbank (rather financial people!), or the All-Ukrainian Cooperative Association, even the Ukrainian Handicraft Association (although it is very sick!), then I am sure that after much deliberation their inevitable resolution would be [...]:

> *'For a ruble and twenty*
> *give us a woman with spunk.'*

. . . .

For the Crimean moon is gracing the sky.

30.5.1924

CRIMEAN SUN

After the night, the Crimean night (Ah night! Ah, Crimean night!), the sun is here!

This is the Crimean sun, appearing from behind the jagged peak of Ay-Petri...

When the inky-blue night takes on an azure milkiness, when the night sheds its shroud, its blue purdah, a deep inky blue, and the sea grabs the purdah and washes it in its crystal-clear waves, rinsing out the blueness, and when the purdah is like the milk from a newly-calved cow and the sea covers itself with it, then the sun appears!

It quietly creeps up to Ay-Petri, without a rustle, and on reaching it, suddenly whacks the mountain's clumsy, jagged head with its golden broom, and shoots up and up the steep azure slope... Running away...

And when Ay-Petri suddenly shakes its shaggy grey head, waving its beard about, and the beard flies off in shreds, and the hair falls away, and the wind blows and old Ay-Petri is left standing bald-headed...! Not a shred of white woolly mist left on its head!

Meanwhile the sun roars with laughter! The sun guffaws! Up above!

And the waves guffaw out at sea too, and the cypresses laugh, and the laurels quake with laughter, and the apricots are all smiles, as well as the grapes and the wellingtonias...

All of Crimea is laughing! Laughing at Ay-Petri...

But Ay-Petri is proud, because it is the highest, the oldest peak... It remains silent...

"Let the children laugh their fill..." it seems to say.

And birds sing, insects buzz joyously, horses neigh, cows swish their tails about faster and, choking, a Crimean donkey tries to 'crow' in a very loud, very abominable voice...

Then the sea is an azure-silver steppe, criss-crossed by blue and white steppe roads, and seagulls sail above, and 'sea swallows'[26] somersault along the roads, carving them up with their sharp tails...

---

26   Dolphins.

Then Crimea sings...

. . . .

The sun rises higher... Higher still...

It's playing... Burning silvery gold, sending generous splashes of hot gold behind and ahead, to the right, and to the left...

And the sea becomes hotter, and the mountains warmer, and the needles of black cypresses rustle in the hot sultry air...

It climbs higher...! Higher still!

And everything living chases after it... The grape stretches its juicy vine toward it, and the cedar pushes into the heavens too, and the tips of the lush wellingtonias strive toward it, trying to reach it...

And the hot sea breathes, sending its breath toward the sun's golden splashes...

And the sun climbs higher! Higher still!

From its unattainable heights, the sun sprinkles its hot vigour over everything, coddling and filling everything with juices, and these juices froth, seethe and run riot...

Those hot juices...

And because of the warmth, Nature bears fruit far more quickly. Cherries ripen before one's very eyes, and peaches turn yellow, and plums swoon...

Because their hot juices are seething! Because these juices are hot...

And only the cornel stands hard and dead.

The cornel is called the 'devil's berry'.

. . . .

...When Allah created the world and finished His work, spring came upon the Earth, and the buds of the trees began to open one after another.

And everything living set upon the buds, and Allah saw that He had to impose some order. So He summoned everyone together and asked them to each choose a tree or a flower, which they would then use exclusively.

Each asked for different things. Then the Devil's turn came.

"Have you decided, Devil?" Allah asked.

"Yes," the Devil replied, screwing up his cunning eyes.

"What have you chosen?"

"Cornel."

"Cornel?! Why cornel?"

"Oh, no reason in particular," the Devil said, evading the question.

"All right, you can have the cornel," Allah smiled.

And the Devil hopped about with joy. He had managed to deceive everyone. The cornel had flowered before all the other trees, so it must ripen before them too. And the first berry of the season was expensive and much sought after. He would take his cornel berries to market and sell them at a hefty profit.

Summer arrived. Fruit began to ripen: cherries, apricots, peaches, apples, pears, but the cornel remained green. The Devil scratched his head in rage...

"Hurry up, ripen!"

But the cornel did not ripen.

The Devil began to blow at the berries, which made them turn a brilliant red, but they remained hard and sour.

"So, how's your cornel going?" the people laughed.

The Devil spat heartily and the cornel turned black...

"Such abominable stuff! I won't take it to market! Collect it yourselves!"

And this they did. After all the fruit had been harvested in the orchards, the people went into the forests to collect the delicious, sweet, blackened cornel berry, and quietly sniggered at the Devil.

"The Devil's let a good opportunity pass!"

The Devil was raging mad and had his revenge on the people... He knew that people were greedy. So he made it that the following autumn the cornel crop was twice as big, and for all the berries to ripen, the sun had to send more warmth than usual upon the Earth.

The people were overjoyed at such a harvest, failing to understand the Devil's ploy.

Meanwhile, the sun had grown tired over summer, and there followed such a cold winter on Earth, that the people's orchards were destroyed by frosts, and they just managed to survive.

From that time, a good crop of cornel berries has been a sure sign of a cold winter to come, for the Devil still hasn't forgiven the people for laughing at him...

. . . .

Everything living accepts the sun's golden fire and feeds on it...

And the sun is generous... Like a fairy-tale hero, it hurls that fire down with all its might... And laughs...

The Crimean sun doesn't shun people either...

It embraces their white, anaemic, emaciated bodies with its golden eyelashes, bores into them with those golden eyelashes and nourishes them, cheers them up, paints them...

And it tickles them so gently. It tickles the cautious... However, it makes fun of the incautious... Sometimes even savagely.

It's always on the lookout from its azure loft for anyone gaping... It sneaks up on them, caressing a little, coddling, lulling the person to sleep... And at the same time, it skins their forehead, their nose and their neck with peals of golden laughter... Removing the skin in sheets. First it coddles, and then paints the skin red, then blisters it and removes it heartlessly...

And then the incautious person fidgets, and snivels, and oohs and ahs, and tosses and turns, and groans.

While the sun laughs away merrily!

Watching from above and roaring with laughter as some milky-soft lady makes her way home from the beach...

The sun has already touched such places on her body that no one else would have ever dared touch...

Felt her all over and left behind boils...

And then she heads for home in such a quaint manner that it's hard for me to even describe it... We need an artist here, our Sashko[27] for example, to capture the hapless lady's predicament...

The poor thing's legs are spread apart like dividers... That which is supposed to protrude, is drawn in, and that which is normally drawn in, is protruding...

And she walks along in such an ungainly fashion, that she looks rather unfeminine...

Because the lady is aching all over... Aching from the sun... The golden-hot Crimean sun...

While the lady's mouth was agape, it had felt her nicely all over!

That golden Crimean sun!

15.6.1924

---

27   I'm referring here to Oleksandr Dovzhenko, a film-maker, but also a very talented artist. Only he can't draw me – comes up with some bald monstrosity, the damned fellow. *O.V.*

MOUNTAINS

Mountains are such tall things... That's just by the by...

The Crimean Mountains are neither too low, nor small, nor short...

[...]

Each mountain individually, and therefore all the mountains collectively, consist of three parts: the foothills, the slopes, and the peak... The foothills are the low part, the slopes are a little further up, and the peak – well that's very high up...

The most difficult part of a mountain to reach is the foothills... Extremely difficult...

Tourists really pride themselves on this.

"I've been on Ay-Petri!"

"The peak or the foothills?"

"The foothills!"

"Good lad! You're a real knight!"

The 'knight' smiles from ear to ear: yes, he made it, after all.

To reach the slopes is much easier. Especially if you're descending from the top, the peak...

And it's really nothing to reach the peak... Just grab hold of a stick, and walk...

And after that you spend two or so weeks in bed: digesting your impressions, so to speak... You rest quietly, peacefully; without moving your arms or legs...

Well, it's no surprise, because to bound up the Babuhan like a gazelle, for instance, gives people much pleasure. 1543 metres up is somewhat higher than Kharkiv's Kholodna Hora[28], (even when you're on the top floor of the city jail!)... You know yourselves what a sight it is to look down on Kharkiv at night from Kholodna Hora... You can see far, and you can see everything... Especially when you're sober and not afraid of being mugged... So it must be quite a sight then from Babuhan, or Chatyr-Dag, or Ay-Petri!

---

28   A hilly southern suburb of Kharkiv, literally means Cold Mountain.

———•———

There are dachas in the foothills. Forests on the slopes. Snows on the peaks. Snows in summer, and snows in winter!

And on the slopes, there are mountain streams.

And in the forests, there are buffalo, wild goats, and 'green'[29] partisans...

Of late, though, the partisans have become extinct... But in Wrangel's[30] time they say there was a plague of them in the mountains... 'Supporting' Baron Wrangel in his sacred duty to rebuild a 'single and indivisible Russia'... A sacred Russia!

———•———

But the most important thing for us mere mortals is the mountain air... There's quite a bit of it here. And you don't need to pay for it – you can just go and breathe it in whenever you feel like it...

Only there's a ban on exporting it. Although some tourists do take a small bag of air from Chatyr-Dag or Babuhan home with them...

The air here is clean, clear, fragrant, fresh...

Of course, this is only if you plod through the mountains alone, without a large group of friends laden with baskets of hard-boiled eggs and sardines, wearing triple-strength cologne and 'Kaloderma' powder and talc to ease the sweating... But if you clamber up Ay-Petri in a group like this, then it's no better than Sumska Street in Kharkiv at nine in the evening. Then even the beech trees sneeze!

———•———

The mountains here are very fearful! Most of them begin with 'Ay':

---

29   Generalized name given to irregular, predominantly peasant armed formations who opposed foreign interventionists, Bolsheviks (Reds) and pro-tsarist (White) forces during the Civil War in Russia.

30   P.M. Wrangel, member of an old German baronial family, was a pro-tsarist, anti-communist Russian general supported by the English, French and Americans, who invaded Crimea in 1920 with 30,000 troops with the intention of overthrowing the Soviet regime and restoring monarchic rule in the Russian Empire.

'Ay-Petri, Ay-Mykola, Ay-Todor, Ay-Ya, etcetera...'

And this, by the way, is contagious...

Very often you hear someone exclaiming, as they climb up the mountains:

"Ay, my God!"

"Ay, mother dear!"

Or simply:

"Oy, don't let go of me!"

"Oy, help!"

8.6.1924

THE BEACH

As you make your way down the slope from Simeiz Park to the sea, there's a signpost at a fork in the path, bearing the inscription:

Men's Beach   Women's Beach

Under 'Men's Beach' there's an arrow pointing this way, and under 'Women's Beach' there's an arrow pointing that way...

This is so that people, feeling male or female as the case may be, don't find themselves where they've no right to be. So that the people lay their bodies out on the hot pebbles precisely where their bodies belong...

The 'orthodox' descend the path to the blue sea without regard to sex or nationality, until they reach this signpost. And when one of the 'orthodox' people is a man, he stops by the signpost and gazes at the women's side, and the poor fellow hesitates, thinking that it would be far less trouble and better for his health to lie precisely over there, where bodies with wide pelvises lie in a heap, with 'nice arrangements' on their chests, quite different from his.

And when a woman descends the path, she glances furtively at the men's side... No, of course women don't think that it would be less trouble and better for their health to lie down over there, where representatives of the stronger sex have stretched out their 'beams', all handsome like Belvederian Apollos, noses facing the sky, with smooth bald skulls and underpants shielding their governmental heads from the sun.

———•———

That's the beach for you.

Sun above, hot pebbles below, sea in front, and naked bodies on the pebbles...

Soviet society bakes here.

Baking discussions, conferences, meetings, resolutions, directives, travelling allowances, purges, staff reductions, the labour exchange and taxes...

Over there a well-tanned bald fellow with a Babylonian-Assyrian beard and a chest as hairy as the biblical Isaiah's has exposed his gastro-intestinal tract, inflated to drum-sized proportions, and is wheezing, and groaning, and fidgeting...

He's probably from a syndicate... What is he baking? Perhaps a worker-peasant inspection, perhaps a subsidized allowance for his 'state' flat and powerful Benz... He lies stoically before the sun's hot spears, turning his Homo sapiens bulk over from stomach to back, and from back to stomach...

He would gladly burn away all the Soviet authority inside him to be able to return to his bank or business office and to work for the restoration of a world's 'national' economy and universal culture...

Occasionally, he jumps up and slowly makes his way across the pebbles to the sea... Wades cautiously into the water, stops, blocks his ears with his thumbs and presses his nostrils flat with his forefingers and yelps:

"Oof!"

He takes a dip in the sea...

Coming up, he shakes his Babylonian-Assyrian beard like a billy-goat, looking around...

Nearby boys are guffawing, their laughter sending waves across the surface. They somersault about like dolphins, dive into the water and quickly swim up to the Assyrian-Babylonian beardo, slapping him on his trust-syndicate backside.

"Ooh, abominable scum! I'll rip your heads off, when I lay my hands on you! Hooligans! You won't be swimming then, you sons-of-bitches!"

The boys are falling over with laughter.

They surround him in a circle, blocking their ears and nostrils with their fingers...

"Petka, can you block one more hole for me, because I haven't enough hands!"

And they exclaim in unison:

"Oof!"

And disappear into the water! Teasing the 'gentleman'.

The hairy belly spits heartily, swears and claws his way back to shore...

Petka suddenly rushes toward him, screaming:

"Whale!"

The 'gentleman' jumps up in horror and collapses on shore...

Meanwhile the boys are already tumbling through the water, yelling and making their way toward a rock rising from the sea, bespattered with white foam...

"Ooh, the rascals!"

———•———

The 'orthodox' lie one beside the other, sunning themselves...

And the sun scalds them...

Groaning, and moaning, and fidgeting, the orthodox people roll over from one side to the other...

Then they jump up, race to the sea and throw themselves into its blue-green waves:

Oof! Oof! Oof!

And they tousle about, splashing and clapping... Grreat!

. . . .

Occasionally a member of the beautiful sex wanders past the men's beach... Her face is covered with a scarf and turned away: but one curious eye keeps peeping out from behind the scarf at the sand – peep! peep!

Interested in the anatomy of the human body.

And sometimes one of the Apollos suddenly finds himself on the women's beach, 'lost in contemplation'. Then towels flap like fans on the women's beach, and everything which constitutes a sacred part of the female anatomy is hurriedly covered...

So that he doesn't cast an evil eye over it!

. . . .

And by the rock over there sits a rickety old man, his moustache twirled up. He is terribly indifferent to everything. And he has come here solely for treatment. Beside him lies a pair of binoculars. And when no one is looking, he hastily brings the binoculars to his eyes and directs them... at the women's beach...

The old grandpa is 'medicating' himself...

. . . .

And on that women's beach some Venus is presently dragging her sensual body from the sea, all 155 kilos of it...

Her 'supple' figure creaks across the pebbles, and the waves crash against her as if she was Virgin Rock[31]...

Poor thing, she must be suffering from the eighteenth stage of consumption...

Dragging herself from the water, she collapses on the shore in a mass of jelly... And breathes heavily, heaving the two pillows on her chest...

She is blocking the horizon...

One itches to say to her in the words of Sasha Cherny:

Madam, your big bum
has obscured the sun...
And the sun is far nicer a view!

01.07.1924

---

31   Coastal limestone rock in the Black Sea near the village of Simeiz in Crimea. Its upper part resembles a woman's bust with loose flowing hair.

SUMMER BY THE RIVER

[...]

It's Sunday...

From the bridge to Trukhaniv Island (when looking from Volodymyr's Hill, it will be on your left) all the way across to Margolin's Dacha, the low left sandy shore is cluttered with bodies. Kyiv's inhabitants are imbibing the sun's energy to utilize it on Monday 'for the revival of the national economy'.

This place is called a beach.

'Lifesavers Beach'...

Thousands of people – men, women and children – lie on the sand and burn away their 'nerves and exhaustion' in the sun...

See those signs:

'Women's Beach'...

'Children's Beach'...

'Men's Beach'...

These are merely signs... No one takes any notice of them any more...

On the 'women's' beach one can see a host of creatures, which no matter how short-sighted one may be, one could never mistake for women...

And no one cares...

Only occasionally a representative of the fair sex will say, more for her own justification than anything else:

"How insolent these men are! There's a beach set aside for them, but no, they insist on crawling over here! One simply can't get away from them!"

And she turns to gawk at the 'insolent fellow', so that even he turns away, practically blushing...

The same goes for the 'children's' beach...

Now here's a 'child' for you.

Stretched out to his full seven feet! Mustache hanging down to his collarbone; one would be able to carve seven children from his right leg alone.

And next to him some representative of the peasant-worker state has rested his paunch... You can't see any arms or legs because of all the fat. It's as if someone has dumped a pile of white manure on the sand... And the part of his anatomy called a face is crumpled up like a dirty handkerchief and whistles methodically... Relaxing on the beach...

And here is the 'men's beach'... At least that's what the sign says...

But no, those can't be men...

Can that be a man in a pink knitted bathing suit with bows on the shoulders...? Not on your life... Skipping along the shoreline and daintily prancing about... Quite unmasculine.

Or take that 'specimen', for example... How can you take that individual for a male, when their 'difference' is ready to burst out the top of their knitted bathing suit and to spill out onto the sandy expanse of the beach...

. . . .

Baskets, umbrellas, straw hats, sheets, bottles, glasses...

And bodies... bodies... bodies...

Nowhere to step...

People bending over, turning about, snoring, shrieking, yelling...

He's lying there peacefully... Then all of a sudden, up he jumps and splashes headlong into the Dnipro River!

"Ah! Ah! Ah! Oh-ho-ho-ho-ho!!!"

And back onto the sand.

Meanwhile the Dnipro River is calm again...

Why should it care?

It has seen its fair share of wonders over the ages...

Occasionally, old man river gives a wriggle and sends a wave rolling to shore...

When some incautious person ventures out further than they can handle, the Dnipro grabs at them... Then you can hear:

"He-e-elp!"

On the first day the beach was opened, the river was agitated...

'So what?' you might say.

It claimed thirty lives, they say...

The river likes sacrifices from time to time...

It can't forget the past...

. . . .

And the sun! The sun! It stings!

Whenever it gets sick of staring at those intertwined bodies, it pops behind a cloud...

There it rests, and then leaps out and flogs the human worms with its golden whip so hard, that they begin to writhe...

What a great sun!

Burning hot, but gentle!

Because if I was to assume its place up there in the sky, I would have long since incinerated that old bag over there with pencilled-in eyebrows who has laid out her wares! I'd have sent those wares of hers up in smoke.

[…]

31.07.1923

THE NEWS (1921)

(Shadows of Unforgotten Ancestors[32])

I

"Comrade Kukuy, bring us some supplies from the printing shop."

"Look, for one thing, that's your own private affair. Secondly, if you keep entrusting me with your private affairs, I'll complain to the Third Congress of the Communist International and to the Fourth Assembly of the People's Commissariat."

Okay, then, sit tight. To hell with you."

"And if I want to remain standing?"

"Then remain standing."

"And if I want to sit down?"

"Will you go to hell?"

"As you wish."

The News has begun work for the day.

II

"Who's this 'Rosta'? Sends us a telegram that apple-trees have blossomed in Sebastopol, and pumpkins have sprouted in Crimea. Tell me, though, is Crimea in Sebastopol or Sebastopol in Crimea?"

"In the Caspian Sea, I think."

"What's in the Caspian Sea?"

"Herrings."

"I was talking about apple trees."

"Can't tell, haven't heard."

"I'll write: 'Miscellaneous'. 'From Abroad'."

The morning's dispatch has arrived.

---

32   A play on the title of Mykhailo Kotsiubynsky's book "Shadows of Forgotten Ancestors".

III

"Hello! You're here already? Why so early?"

"It was three o'clock when I looked. Seemed a bit early, I thought I'd be finished by twelve."

"We've been working hard since eleven yesterday."

"Good. Want me to come back at four?"

"Here, translate this."

"Boy, I could do with some *kvas* now."

"I wouldn't mind a chunk of bacon fat."

"Why bacon fat?"

"How do you say 'nose' in Ukrainian?"

"*Nis.*"

"*Nis*? You replace the 'o' in Russian with an 'i' and they already think it's another language."

"*Vukho's* better. 'Ear' is the same in both languages."

"Then write '*vukho*'!"

...The translator hard at work...

IV

"Stasyk! Sta-a-a-a-asyk!"

"You call him, you've got a nice deep voice!"

"Hrm! Hrm! Sta-a-asyk!"

"Kostya, darling, where's Stasyk?"

"Excushe me, Comrade Shtam, where'sh Shtashyk?"

"One minute? Maria Albertovna, where's Stasyk?"

"Just a moment! Maria Nikolayevna, where's Stasyk?"

"Oh, my God! Anna Yosifovna, where's Stasyk?"

"Comrades! One-two-three...! All together now."

"...Sta-a-a-asyk!"

"I'm-a here!"

"Where you been hiding?"

"I was with the boys. One of 'em plays cards splendidly. He's just amazing! Each time he throws down a card he lets out such a gasp!"

"All right, get this to the printer's... Does he really play so splendidly?"

"My oath."

"Well, hurry up, then."

...Our courier.

V

"Comrade! It's Ivan Franko's anniversary tomorrow. Slap us something together! I feel quite uncomfortable. After all – it's Franko!"

"All right, but I'll do it on Shevchenko's[33] anniversary. Then I'll write one article about the pair of 'em. There's no time now."

"Oh well, all right."

The Cultural-Arts Department at work.

VI

"Comrade production editor, will you be coming in today?"

"Don't know, I'll probably be shick. I had shuch a gumboil yeshterday, shuch a gumboil. My right leg puffed up so much, I couldn't put my glove on. Not sure about today, I'll probably come down with typhus."

"But, comrade, you are bound by Party discipline."

"Maybe, bound by Party discipline, I'll become shick. And it's not fair, anyway. I've released the newspaper some five times in the past six months, and it hasn't released me even once."

"Well, okay."

...Our production editor.

VII

"No, Pavel Mikhailovich, that's disgraceful. See, it says clearly here in the telegram that the events took place in a Far-Eastern republic. So I wrote 'In Upper Silesia', but it was shoved in under 'The Sowing Campaign'. That's seditious. It says in the telegram that the Japanese Army has withdrawn from Siberia, so I gave the headline 'Coal Miners Continue to Resist', and they typeset 'Marusia Poisons Herself', when I know only too well that

---

33   Ivan Franko (1856-1916), revolutionary Ukrainian poet and writer; Taras Shevchenko (1814-1861) is still lauded as the most influential poet in Ukraine's history.

Marusia still operates in Zaporizhia District near Pereyaslav. I simply can't stand this any more."

"It's quite all right, Lidia Mykhailivna, it's quite all right!"

...The evening dispatch.

VIII

"Comrade, where you off to?"

"The editorial office. It's already time."

"Turn back."

"Why?"

"They're bathing little Marusia[34] in the editor's office. And the little devil keeps splashing water everywhere. [...]

"Maybe we could do it in your office?"

"No, the nappies are drying in there. Go home. We'll do it tomorrow."

"So you say they're bathing her and she's splashing water everywhere?"

"Aha. And she's such a cutie. Are you married?"

"Nah."

IX

"Comrade, will there be an editorial?"

"Is the paper coming out?"

"Not without an editorial, it isn't."

"Then why bother about an editorial?"

"What do you mean, why? 'Cause it can't come out without an editorial."

"If it's not coming out, then there's no need for an editorial."

"How can you say that?"

"Easy."

"Oh well, all right."

X

"Comrade editor! Can you finally tell me what position I hold here? Is it secretary, make-up man or Kostusia?"

---

34   Daughter of the commissar of the printing shop – *O.V.*

"How am I supposed to know?"

"Kostusia comes up to me yesterday and says in Polish: 'Excuse me, mister secretary, open your mouth, please.'

"'What for?' I asked.

"'So I can fill you full of water. Because mister editor said that you'll be our samovar from now on.'

"I have nothing against that, of course. I might even boil over. But how are you going to draw water from me? At least attach a tap to me."

XI

"Has the newspaper come out?"

"No, not yet."

"Why?"

"Because Kostusia didn't turn the samovar on."

"Excushe me. It's not my fault. Mister secretary wouldn't open his mouth."

. . . .

I must comment though, that this was written back in the time and about those times, when the appointed editor and secretary were on holidays (May-June 1921), and the acting editor was comrade N..., before whom I take this opportunity to curtsy...

Kharkiv, 1921

COOPERATIVE MATTERS

The cooperative is the path to socialism...

Well, some not very nice people have gone and built a Central Workers Cooperative restaurant at 3 Karl Libknecht Street and a Central Workers Co-operative grocery store at 11 Roza Luxembourg Square...

This is here in Kharkiv.

And these establishments are scaring away the working folk and travellers are bypassing this socialist path, deviating from it and running along the path to true capitalism, without letting anyone utter a single word.

"Shut up!" they shout. "Listen to what's happening first, before you tell us off."

"So I'm all ears..."

"Well then... I went conscientiously along the path to cooperation... Public dining, I thought... The emancipation of women... Let's go to the Central Workers Cooperative restaurant, honey, I said to my wife... It's in new premises... There's music... Flowers... And we went there... Sat down... Remained seated... I read the 'Evening Radio'... We ate the bread on the table... We were sitting in our coats... It became stuffy, so we took them off... We listened to about five lyrical songs... At last the waiter arrived."

"Here for lunch?"

"Yes, please," we said.

"What would you like?"

"Borsch for me."

"Soup for me," said the wife.

"One minute..."

We sat there. My wife told me about her eight years at high school... She recounted in great detail about each of the eight years. I told my wife about the Civil War, about events in China, the state grain purchase, exports and the Locarne conference. We finished a second plate of bread...

"Borsch for you, and soup for you?"

"No," I said, "borsch for me, soup for her..."

"One minute..."

We continued to sit there. We speculated for a long time how much insurance people would have to pay after the construction of houses became widespread in Kharkiv.

"Here you are, two borsches... What would you like for main course?"

"We ordered one borsch and one soup..."

"My apologies! One minute."

"No, matey, we'll take the two borsches... Otherwise the buses will stop running soon... Only please bring us each a spoon and a fork, because you've given us three knives for some reason... Despite your 'one minute', we're not about to start stabbing anyone..."

"One minute!"

. . . .

Now we go to the capitalist *Germany* dining hall and have lunch in fifteen minutes... This is what happens when it comes to having lunch...

And this is what happens when it comes to shopping... Listen...

"I'm all ears..."

I needed to buy some French rolls. I walked into the shop of the Central Workers Cooperative in Roza Luxembourg Square.

"Four rolls, please," I asked.

"One minute."

He handed me four rolls.

"Could you wrap them in paper," I said, "so I can carry them home? Because I've got a long way to go..."

The shop assistant gave me a teeny scrap of paper.

"That's all that's allowed," he said in Russian.

"How am I supposed to take them?" I asked. "They won't fit in my briefcase, and I can't carry them under my arm, I'll lose them along the way..."

"We're not allowed to give any more..."

I left the rolls on the counter, saying:

"Keep your rolls!"

And I crossed the street to the Azerbaijani private bread shop and bought four rolls... And the Azerbaijani gave me a beautiful, large, clean paper bag... And I left with the bag and didn't lose any rolls on the way home...

So judge for yourself now.

Who's to blame, that I'm being scared off the socialist path?

And I ask too:
"Who's to blame?"

29.10.1925

141

TRAVELLING ABROAD

Ulcers don't occur without a reason.

To travel abroad, thus, it seems, you need to have a reason.

Of late, scientific missions have lost some of their influence.

You front up, for example, to an institution which has the right to send you on a mission abroad, and you say:

"You know, it's about time I upgraded my knowledge. The way my research is going, I'm lost without experience abroad. Send me on a mission abroad, and strike me dead if I don't complete the construction of socialism in two weeks. One, two – and there's your socialism for you!"

And, of course, you show them a certificate from the institute you work at, where it says that you really do need to go abroad. Just as you need overtime, water and air to survive.

Then the institution replies:

"Yeah... We can see that you really need to go abroad. But take into consideration, comrade, the findings of our experts. Soviet-produced women's stockings and shoes are no worse than those made abroad. And taking import duty into account, they're not more expensive. Also, you may only bring back two suits. Therefore, when you consider the cost of the trip, the duty, the high cost of living abroad, you don't gain that much... And they don't issue import licences anymore. And to wrap women's underwear and lace around yourself is uncomfortable, besides you'll appear on the newsreel then. And you won't succeed in bringing in hard currency, because customs can tell at a glance who's carrying hard currency..."

"Ah, yes... Well, I'll think about it then..."

"Yeah, think about it..."

A far better and more valid reason for travelling abroad is illness.

It's easier to leave the country if you're ill...

Only don't do what a lady friend of mine did.

She fainted in front of the medical commission, where she turned up for a certificate stating that she required treatment abroad. When they gave her smelling salts, she came to, and began to groan:

"Oh! Where am I? And what can you bring back from abroad? I've been told you have such a list. Oh! Oh!"

And she fainted again.

Don't go about it that way – you'll definitely fail.

The surest way to get permission to travel abroad is to get a nice stomach ulcer. A nice round ulcer.

How do you acquire them? I'll tell you some other time when I have a free moment. You'll get a really fine ulcer…

. . . .

At last you've got your foreign travel passport. Everyone knows about it.

"Going abroad?"

"Yeah."

"Well, you know, get me a fountain pen."

"All right."

"Going abroad?"

"Yeah."

"Perhaps you could get me a broad-rimmed hat."

"All right."

. . . .

"Get me three or so ties then."

"All right."

. . . .

"Eh, they've got some really great toys over there. I wouldn't mind a little bike for my Yurko and a teddy-bear for Marynka. Only one of those big ones. They have these really furry ones."

. . . .

"Going?"

"Yeah."

"Great. Boy, what luck. Thank God for the ulcer. Well, get us something there too. Some note pads. Pocket-knives. And those self-propelling pencils. And some socks."

"My wife begged you to get her a jumper and a pair of Lisle-thread stockings…"

"Comrades! Maybe someone would like a grand piano? Or maybe a car?"

Sitting in the railway carriage you look in your note pad and tally up what you must bring back from abroad.

The totals: 13 hats, 45 ties, 23 pairs of shoes, 110 pairs of stockings, 87 fountain pens, 15 dozen pencils, 5 bicycles, 7 teddy-bears...

You see black spots before your eyes, and looking out over the green fields of rye, you think stubbornly:

'Well, all right! I'll wrap some of it round myself! Stuff a few things in my shoes! And the bicycles I'll check in with the luggage! But where can I shove those teddy-bears?'

. . . .

Dear customs officers in Shepetivka! When I crawl out of the train ten times as fat as when I left the country, please think it's weight I've put on in a German sanatorium. And when you see teddy-bears sticking out of my ears and hats from my nose, please think that the doctors prescribed that I block all my openings.

Well, what else can I do?! I'm going abroad!

. . . .

We're on our way.

"Now look, comrade: 'Raucher' is for smokers, 'Nichtraucher' is for non-smokers."

"How do you say 'second class'?"

"Zweiter Klasse. Say just that at the station."

"Who to?"

"To whoever asks you."

"Aha. Yikh khabe tsvaiter klyasse. Yikh khabe tsvaiter. Yikh khabe tsvaiter..."

"At the station look for a sign which says 'Ausgang', and go out there. 'Ausgang' means exit."

"Aha... How do you say exit again?"

"Ausgang."

"Aha. Ausgang... ausgang... ausgang... My, what a difficult word..."

"And when you arrive, there'll be a sign 'Bahnhof Friedrichstrasse'. That's where you get off the train. 'Bahnhof' means station, 'Strasse' means street. Get off there."

"Aha, then. 'Yikh khabe tsvaiter klyasse'. 'Ausgang' means station. 'Bahnhof' means exit. Aha."

"No, it's the other way around"

"What d'you mean? 'Yikh khabe tsvaiter klyasse' means station?"

"No."

"Aha. 'Bahnhof' means station."

"Zwanzig. Dreizig. Vierzig. And what do I do after that 'ausgang'?"

"Ask someone for directions."

Ask someone. All right, I'll ask someone. How we'll do the asking is another thing, but ask we must.

At last we're on our way... At last... At last...

Shepetivka...

You know, as you near Shepetivka, you begin to feel kind of queasy. It's not that you'll have to pass through customs... Customs is only customs... What can customs demand from our man when he's travelling abroad? Nothing.

They set out on their mission with the barest of essentials. One of our fellow travellers was full of regret:

"Pity you can't travel abroad naked. You could bring back so much more."

And I said to him:

"You should rub yourself all over with ash, fix two to three cheap bras to your body, and travel like that. And if anyone were to ask, you reply: 'This is our uniform.'"

No, it's nothing to do with customs.

As you near Shepetivka, you have a growing urge to turn back. To hop off the train and dart back to Kyiv. Once you cross Shepetivka, you're all alone... On your lonesome... And the dearest thing you have left is your red passport... And you reach for it with your free hand every five minutes.

In case—God forbid!—it should fall out. Because then you're a goner.

When you're between Shepetivka and Zdolbuniv, there's dead silence in the carriage.

Why is it so quiet? It's as if everyone's returning from a funeral.

The border patrol leaves the train. And you long for them so badly, as if they were your own brothers.

The neutral zone...

'Mohyljany'. White eagles everywhere. And the station platforms are empty... Mohyljany Station.

"Please, sir, your passport!"

You look around... "Who's the knight around here?" you think to yourself.

A man is looking you straight in the face. He's wearing a black helmet with a white eagle on the front, and he addresses you as 'sir'.

Looks like I'm a knight, after all. How quickly! Only some ten kilometres and I'm already a 'knight'!

We're in Poland.

01.7.1928

THE CORRUPTION OF THE BOURGEOISIE

It's not surprising, comrades, that when our man finds himself in a large European city, the first thing he does is run off to view the corruption of the bourgeoisie.

Some of you will probably shake your heads reproachfully:

"Ah, the so-and-so! Don't worry, he didn't hit the workers' quarters to see how the Western European workers live and work! No, he made for the dance halls and cabarets to look at the naked bourgeoisie!"

Dear comrades! Please understand us foreign travellers: we are all keen to see the agony, the last minutes, the last throes of the class enemy.

What if this enemy should corrupt away and die?

What a pity it will be that you had the opportunity to see its dying screams and didn't!

So that's why it's the first place that you go.

To see for yourself how the bourgeoisie is perishing:

'Doing the Charleston and drowning in champagne!'

As for the proletariat, there'll still be time to observe its lifestyle and work, because the proletariat is the future.

The reason?

That's just it!

There's a lot of bourgeoisie abroad.

Which is why there are countless pubs in the cities where this bourgeoisie degenerates.

In Berlin, for instance, at every step, almost in every street you can see a cafe, a bar or a restaurant, where the bourgeoisie dance day and night to the sounds of jazz bands, their thin and corpulent bodies sensually intertwined.

On top of this, each street has its cabaret as well, where on a small stage you are shown naked women in different stages of undress.

I haven't seen any dance halls where they show naked men.

Though I suppose they must have them. Really, why deprive yourself of the pleasure of seeing a hefty Belvederian Apollo with a luxuriant growth of hair on his chest, belly and legs!

There's a street in Berlin called Jagerstrasse.

Now then, when you walk down the street around nine or ten in the evening, sleek 'young men' accost you from both sides of the street, shoving leaflets into your hands and importunately asking you to enter their joint, because they've got the best 'fraus'.

The leaflets are illustrated with a nude woman in an appropriate pose.

Well, they talk you into it. And you go in.

A small hall crammed with tables.

A jazz band.

A small raised platform for the performers.

A handful of people.

Cabaret numbers alternate with musical numbers.

Cabaret numbers are women naked from all sides.

A naked woman by herself.

Two naked women.

A lot of naked women at once.

Of course, they're not completely naked, there are still places covered with something special, but ninety percent is unquestionably naked flesh.

Clothed women sit on sofas against the walls.

Naked women on the stage either dance, or exercise, or sing, or simply sway about, showing off their plasticity.

During intermission, when the stage is free of naked women and the band is playing, the clothed women who were sitting against the walls dance some kind of step in between the tables.

I don't know the name of the step. Maybe it's the Charleston or the foxtrot or some other pussy-footing, only it looks, as one old woman put it:

"For forty years I've been married and I didn't know what the foxtrot was about until now!"

Apart from the abovementioned, the hall is filled with a terrible yawning boredom.

Oh, what boredom!

Like a black mist!

Those naked Venuses want to sway about on the stage as much as I want to stick to my diet.

They sway about non-stop from six at night till three in the morning.

Back home our girls weed beets with about as much enthusiasm!

When they come out to do their various naked hocus-pocuses, their faces are so 'cheerful', as if each of them had just buried her most beloved child.

Their legs rise mechanically above their heads, their bodies sway mechanically to the beat of the music, and their faces and thoughts are far from erotica, plasticity, and above all, the cabaret.

Their thoughts are probably back in their apartment, where a mother is waiting for them, where the rent has to be paid, and you have to eat, drink, struggle and survive!

The floor show has finished.

The band begins a dance tune.

Watch the head waiter now.

Watch him closely!

You'll notice how he appears in one corner and stares at the girls sitting against the wall. His eyes meet those of a girl and he nods toward the dance floor:

'Go and dance!'

The girl rises unwillingly, takes her friend by the hand, they trudge to the centre of the hall and begin to dance.

Meanwhile the head waiter tries to catch the attention of another twosome.

Two or three more couples venture out onto the dance floor.

How do they dance?

I watched them and thought:

'It seems that oxen aren't the only ones who ruminate. Looks like you can ruminate by dancing!'

Really, there's no way you could call it dancing!

They crawl about the room like sleepy flies, shuffling their feet, running their eyes over the audience in case someone winks and offers them a glass of coffee, at the very least.

Oh, how very merry!

So merry, so merry, that if you stayed here a few days longer, you'd come back home, climb the Cossack Cliffs on the Donets River and jump headlong into the water below. [...]

We sat in one of these cabarets. They even had two orchestras playing.
One was a jazz band and the other a balalaika ensemble.

The balalaika players all wore Russian *kosovorotka*[35] shirts.

I don't know whether they were emigres or just locals dressed up. The balalaika players strummed some dance tunes as well, because couples crawled around the dance floor to their music too.

And they also sang.

The ensemble sang.

Lord Almighty! I've been at birthdays, christenings, church services, funerals, but nowhere have I heard people sing so terribly.

I'm not referring to their voices, I mean their performance.

You get the impression that someone stubborn and callous has grabbed each musician by the colon, wound all their intestines around his hand and is now pulling on them ever so slowly.

This stubborn, callous guy pulls slowly at the guts, the pain is excruciating and the performers howl.

When the torturer gives a tug, they all let out a scream, when he lets go and then begins to pull slowly again, they continue their hopeless and sorrowful howling.

Makes you want to call out:

"Hey, old chap, let go of their guts, will you! Stop torturing the poor people! Give them at least a minute's rest. Let them stop and catch their breaths! Let go-o-o!"

But he doesn't relent... And they continue to 'sing'.

When the music and singing stop, the sleepy flies crawl back to the sofas and begin to shoot streamers at the guests.

You think that's playfulness?

No! That's the owner making more money. He sends his 'flies' to sell streamers to the guests.

Well, the guests buy them and the 'flies' then shoot the streamers at the guests.

They toss the streamers reluctantly, tediously, slowly.

And when the hall becomes entangled in thin multi-coloured streamers, the streamers remind you so much of a cobweb, and the face of the owner-spider peers from the web, keeping a predatory eye on the entangled fly-girls.

---

35   A typically Russian shirt with slit in the front made off to one side and not in the middle, as with most shirts.

Guests?

In my opinion, Germans make dull guests.

The damned tsarist Russian merchants were experts at such things: they broke mirrors, daubed the waiters with mustard and turned the piano into an aquarium.

But Germans are quite the opposite!

A German orders a glass of Mineralwasser or coffee and sits on it for hours, sucking on his cigar.

He is rather cold-blooded – naked flesh does not quicken his pulse.

There are a lot of grandpas among the guests.

Mangy, ancient men covered in wrinkles, lower lips trembling.

So what of them?

The old fellow can't shake much more than his lower lip.

Well, the old fellow sits and champs his lips, his head nodding away. And that's all! No more!

Sometimes one of them grabs his right eyebrow and gives it a tug (since it can't move of its own accord). Then a 'fly' settles down beside him.

She sits down...

In an instant, others gather 'round like vultures: with chocolates, streamers, flowers, cigars. And the head waiter sidles up with a wine list and the snack menu.

In most cases this 'attack' comes to naught.

The old codger orders nothing, because he can't rise to more than platonic love.

So boring...

They say that all these dance halls and cabarets cater almost exclusively to foreigners.

Maybe that's so?

But are foreigners really so melancholy that they will be interested and satisfied with such a flytrap filled with naked women?

I always thought that the bourgeoisie corrupted more merrily.

Perhaps I could make a suggestion: if that's how you're going to corrupt, better wait a while, until people are found who can corrupt you more quickly and merrily. At least you won't be so sad then.

. . . .

So sad!

18.7.1928

BERLIN'S MUSEUMS

It is of uttermost importance, you know, to see the museums! To be in Berlin and not visit the museums is an out and out crime! Berlin's museums are the quintessence of all museums... You know what German culture is? Well, in the museums they've amassed the whole lot! From the most ancient times. From the time the Germans invented the monkey to the present day! Tomorrow morning, straight after breakfast, we'll do the rounds of the museums.

"We'll only visit the museums! Soon as we get up, we'll go and visit the museums. Why on earth come here, if you don't visit the museums?"

"Hurry up with breakfast and we'll be off! Come on!"
"One minute! I'll just swallow this cheese and we'll be off!"
"Let's go, let's go, the museums close at three."
"Off we go!"

"We're off."
"Faster, faster, comrade! The museums are vast and we haven't much time!"
"Just look at this! Come here! Look at the beautiful suitcase! And the lovely shop window!"
"What a case! Mamma-mia! Look, it's more like a whole wardrobe! And a compartment for everything. Jackets over here, pants there, underwear there! Nothing'll crease in a suitcase like that. I'll have to buy one!"
"How much is it?"
"There's a toiletry case over there! See?"
"Yeah! What a beauty!"
"I simply must get one! And over there, see, real crocodile skin!"
"Where?"
"There! There! I really must get one!"
"Look here, a reticule! Red too! Oh, hell! I really need one!"
"C'mon, c'mon, let's go! We'll be late!"
"Let's go!"

"Psst! Look at those bananas! My, what bananas!"

"No, those pineapples are better!"

"What are those red berries?"

"Those? God only knows what they are! And there's a watermelon, or some such."

"No, doesn't look like one."

"What is it then?"

"No idea! But look at those cherries! Big as tomatoes!"

"They are tomatoes!"

"No, they're cherries!"

"What the hell! I must buy some!"

"C'mon, c'mon, let's go!

"Full steam ahead!"

"Listen, what's that monster over there? A crocodile or something?"

"It's an inflatable rubber crocodile!"

"What the hell for?"

"They swim on them. See the froggy over there?"

"Some toy or something, is it?"

"Why, yeah! And there are some rubber masks!"

"Are those rubber shoes?"

"They're for swimming too."

"Must get some!"

"C'mon, let's go!"

"Yeah, hurry along!"

"What's that, a live mannequin or something?"

"Why, yeah! It's the latest rage. They've got special ladies that dress up and stand in shop windows to advertise clothing!"

"Not a bad little mannequin! Must get one!"

"C'mon, let's run!"

"I'm coming, I'm coming!"

"Look here! Imitation pearls! My wife told me about them!"

"Yeah, that's them all right! That's them!"

"Just you look at 'em, will you?"

"There's better ones over here!"

"Hey, look at the snake! What's it made of?"

"Probably terracotta!"
"We'll have to pop in here! See that necklace?"
"Wow!"
"I must get one!"
"Let's hurry!"
"Let's!"

"Look at those small electric lights, will you?"
"Blue, pink and red ones! There's millions of them!"
"Take a look at these, they flash on and off!"
"Gee!"
"Boy, look at these lanterns!"
"There's enough stuff here to fit out a whole power station!"
"Wow! Must get some!"
"C'mon, let's go, it's already twelve!"
"Let's go!"

"Aha-ah-aha! I simply must pop into this shop! See the coat with that lining!"
"I need one too! It's just the thing I've been looking for!"
"No, let's shop around first! The one over there's worth a hundred and twenty marks!"
"That's nothing! Here's a better one for a hundred and fifty!"
"Just what I need for work!"
"Hey, they've got shoes here too!"
"Why, it's a sporting goods shop!"
"A-a-ah! Sport! Pity I don't play football, I'd have bought those boots! Oh, what boots, you can tell they're good quality!"
"C'mon, let's not dawdle. It's twelve-thirty!"
"Off we go!"

"Here's those fountain pens! And look! A new kind! Haven't seen any of these around before!"
"Those green ones? They're American!"
"I need quite a few of 'em, you know! One for Mykola, and Fedir, and Sydir, and Ivan, and Viktor, and more, and more, and more... I've forgotten how many I need. About ninety or so. You reckon they'll give a discount on bulk purchases? Eh?"

"We'll have to ask!"

"They've got note pads too! And pencils! We'll have to remember this shop! What's it called? I'd better jot it down so we don't forget."

"All right, but hurry up there, we really have to get a move on!"

"Right, let's fly!"

"Hey, look at that. A live horse being driven around in a car!"

"Aha! They're probably taking him to the races! Don't want him to tire on the way."

"Well, I never – horses getting about in cars! Wonders never cease! And the devil's as cool as a cucumber. Used to it, I suppose."

"C'mon, let's go! C'mon!"

"What's that stuffed dummy in white?"

"That's a cook from the restaurant advertising the place! It says across his stomach which restaurant he's from."

"And he stands like that all day long?"

"All day long!"

"My! I must get one!"

"Oh look, watches!"

. . . .

"Oh look, razors!"

"Oh! Oh! Oh! Oh!"

"C'mon, let's get a move on! Here's the museum at last!"

"Look, it's closed!"

"What time is it?"

"Three-thirty!"

"Ah, hell – we're late! And we seemed to be walking quite fast!"

"Well, tomorrow we'll make it for sure! We'll get up early and fly here!"

"Yes, yes! Definitely!"

The next day.

"Hurry-hurry!"

"Just a moment!"

. . . .

"Oh, look, lingerie!"

. . . .
"Oh! Oh! Oh! Oh!"
"What time is it?"
"Quarter past three!"

. . . .

German culture is real culture.
German museums are world famous!
To miss seeing German museums is a crime!
. . . .
"Well, tomorrow for sure!"

31.7.1928

HOW TO GET THROUGH CUSTOMS

When you are travelling abroad you don't have to worry about customs, of course.

But on the way back...

Oh, my God, the price you have to pay because of customs!

About three weeks before leaving Germany the talk begins:

"Everything's fine, but once we reach Shepetivka..."

. . . .

"Been to Tiergarten?"

"Yeah."

"And how d'you like it? A fabulous park, don't you think?"

"Marvellous place. But I don't know whether customs frisk your pockets."

. . . .

"Come from Potsdam?"

"Yes!"

"Wilhelm wasn't mad when he chose to live there. What a park! And the rooms! The fountains! The cleanliness! The order everywhere!"

"Yeah! Makes you wonder. But do customs really let through only one pair of shoes?"

. . . .

"Been to the museum?"

"Just got back."

"Impressive?"

"Superb! Do they let men bring back talcum powder?"

. . . .

"Oh, what a hassle this customs business is!"

They let you bring back so frightfully few things from abroad. Such a harsh limit on everything, makes you want to cry.

Just think – only three suits allowed.

Only two coats.

Just six pairs of underwear.

Only one gold cross and a small gold icon.

Only one string of pearls and one watch.

What a government.

In the instruction form it says you can bring in articles required for personal use over a period of two to three months.

Doesn't the Soviet government know you can't manage with only one watch?

You need three at the very least!

How can any scientific, literary, cultural or industrial worker spend a month abroad with only three suits?

And how can one string of pearls be enough?

Will a worker really be able to visit all those German factories, if he's only allowed to sniff on five hundred grams (half a litre) of *Coty* perfume, which needs to be opened? Mind you, the weight includes the glass bottle.

You just can't make sense of Soviet policy in this instance.

How can it be so?

I set out on the long journey from Berlin to Kharkiv and I can't take a teddy-bear with me?

But it's one of the most essential things.

Am I supposed to travel without being able to cuddle up to my teddy? What sort of a trip is that?

But customs in Shepetivka won't let teddy-bears through.

They declare that it's 'not allowed'...

Pockets are a real tragedy.

For some reason the Germans have very small pockets in their suits.

Shove a teddy-bear in feet first – and his head pokes out.

Shove him in head first – and his feet stick out.

Sit down, make a sudden move, and the devil lets out a howl.

And everyone about you roars with laughter.

What's so funny?

A person travelling abroad on assignment is never so worried and nervous as when he is returning home.

I mean, really, why worry when you arrive in Germany or France?

What can make you anxious there? A new foreign city, new people, different lifestyle, different culture?

You grow used to all this very quickly...

The trepidation begins just before the departure 'nach Hause'.

. . . .

"Excuse me, but aren't you wearing a pair of women's drawers?"

"Can you really tell? I've removed the elastic. Men wear short ones like this in summer these days."

"But they don't have large chrysanthemums sewn onto the front. And another thing, as far as I can recall, men's drawers have a fly, don't they?"

"Why, will customs be looking for flies as well? Why do you keep bringing up Shepetivka customs? I don't want to wear the same clothes as the Shepetivka officials. There are no rules that stipulate I must wear drawers without chrysanthemums!"

. . . .

The pain and suffering that science and scholarship cause our people! The worries a trip abroad creates for our scientists, young and old alike!

Shepetivka. Summer. A real heat wave.

The train carriages disgorge young, red-faced citizens dressed in seal-skin mantles and fur hats, with plush plaid about their necks or in their hands, wearing warm gloves and two or three pairs of woollen underwear...

"Why are you so wrapped up there? Off to the North Pole?"

"I'm scared I might catch cold. The carriages are drafty, you know... My mother had severe rheumatism, she suffered something terrible!"

Shepetivka customs officials are a jovial lot.

When a 'polar explorer' appears before customs, every muscle in the official's face spells mirth.

I saw the consequences of their cheerful nature after they interviewed one such 'sealskin madam'.

On the table lay a string of pearls at least seven metres long, a flagon with no less than a gallon of perfume, heaps of all kinds of lace and stacks of other things.

I would have felt uncomfortable asking her where she had managed to hide it all on her person.

In under half an hour the 'sealskin madam' had lost an enormous amount of weight and had a much paler complexion.

Customs officials with their smiling faces are the worst tormentors...

They're nasty monsters...

They're not moved by tears, or flirting, or serious arguments to the effect that a lady's silk outfit is a must for a young engineer working in the coal mines of Donbas.

Their most cherished phrase is: 'Not allowed.'
A deadly phrase.
And all because of that damned small word 'not'.

Well, all the same, how do you get through customs?
I won't tell you! It's a very big secret.
I passed with flying colours.
I even managed to dupe the officials and sneaked in a life-sized rubber camel.
How?
I stuffed it into the sole of my shoe.
They never tore the soles off my shoes – so I smuggled it in.
Now I don't know what to do with the damned thing – it won't fit in my apartment, the kids are afraid of it, and my wife won't stop cursing me:
"Why couldn't you have stuffed a sealskin mantle into your shoe?"
I agree, I made a mistake there. These things happen.

09.09.1928

MY AUTOBIOGRAPHY

I haven't the slightest doubt that I was born, though during my appearance into the world, and then perhaps for another ten years after that mother maintained that I was pulled out of the well when they were watering our cow Oryshka.

This event occurred on November 14th, 1889 in the town of Hrun, Zinkiv District, Poltava Province. Actually, the event did not take place in the town itself, but in Chechva Settlement near Hrun, on the estate of Landlord von Rot, for whom my father worked as a steward.

Conditions for my development were ideal: on one side, there was a cradle hung from the ceiling, on the other were mother's breasts. I sucked a little, slept a little, and grew up slowly. I was the second child. Before me came my elder brother, who preceded me by one and a half years.

And so it went then: eating-growing, then growing-eating.

My parents were like any parents. My father was male, my mother female. Mother and father had parents too.

Father's father was a cobbler in Lebedyn and drank vodka. Mother's father was a farmer in Hrun and drank vodka too.

I was unable to trace my genealogy any further. Father was not very keen on talking about relatives, and whenever you asked granny (father's mother) about grandfather or some great-grandfather, she inevitably replied:

"They were all scoundrels, just like you! Gave no one any peace! Died from vodka, God rest their souls!"

Of mother's relatives I know equally little. All I remember is father often telling mother:

"You're not like your mother at all, my dove. Is that the way to drink? God rest her soul, your mother loved to drink and knew how to drink."

There was no talk at all about grandfather (mother's father). Obviously, they didn't like the old man. Much later I learned that he had tried to hang himself, but without success, and had gone and died from delirium tremens.

But, on the whole, my parents were alright. Compatible. In their twenty-four years of married life, the Lord sent them only seventeen children, for they knew how to pray to the Almighty.

Whenever a neighbour hinted to father:

"Isn't it about time you stopped the kids, Mykhailo?"

Father would reply:

"There's no need to worry! The Lord gave us children, He'll help us provide for them too."

Father died in 1909, in the fifty-eighth year of his fruitful life.

And at times mother would reminisce about him:

"How long has it been, children, since our father passed away?"

"Oh, close on ten years, mum."

Mother would become pensive and then announce:

"You'd have had another six or so brothers and sisters by now. And I would have had altogether... How many?"

"Twenty-three, mum."

"E-heh! Twenty-three... Oh-ho-ho! May God rest your departed father's soul."

And so I began to grow.

"He'll be a writer," father said once, when I was running my fingers through a puddle on the floor.

As you can see, father's prophecy came true.

But there's no hiding the truth – a lot of time was to pass before father's prediction became fact.

A writer doesn't simply grow up and live like ordinary people.

Ordinary people? They live, live, and then die!

But not a writer. With a writer you are obliged to mention what influenced his outlook on life, what his environment was like, what motivated him even as he lay attached to his mother's tits, champing his lips, completely oblivious to the fact that one day he might have to write his own autobiography.

And now you have to sit and think what influenced you to become a writer, what misfortune dragged you into literature, when you began to wonder about such things as 'where do the holes in doughnuts disappear when you eat them?'

Because authors don't just appear.

And when you reminisce about your life, you come to the conclusion that unusual phenomena accompany an author throughout his entire life, original phenomena, and had these phenomena not been present, you would have perhaps become a decent engineer, a doctor, or simply a clever cooperative manager. The phenomena leap up and you jot them down.

———

Nature generally plays the main role in the formation of a future writer, and for Ukrainian authors, potato plants, hemp and weeds play an important part in their formation.

When a baby boy or girl has a tendency to become engrossed in thought, and they are surrounded by potato plants, or weeds, or hemp – then Bob's your uncle! You can rest assured, they'll become writers.

And quite understandably so. When a child becomes engrossed in thought and squats down on its bare backside, do you think it will be allowed to have a proper think?

Its mother immediately hollers at the top of her voice:

"Where've you sat down, you little sonofabitch!? Isn't there enough room for you behind the pig-pen!"

And the child is forced to rise immediately. And all the inspiration is frightened out of it.

This is where potato plants come in useful.

And so it was with me. Not far behind the house there was a patch of potatoes, further on – hemp. You squatted, the wind rustled past, the sun warmed you, the potato plants inspired thoughts about the universe, the cosmos and socialism.

And you kept thinking and thinking . . .

Until mother yelled:

"Melashka, go and check if Pavlo hasn't fallen asleep out there? But be careful, don't frighten him, so he doesn't shit all over his shirt. I can't keep up with the washing!"

That's what started it. That's what set me thinking. Squatting and scooping out a hole, always intrigued by the depths.

And mother would curse:

"What devil's been digging up the potatoes? The monster can't sit still for a moment. Wait till I catch him!!"

Impulses alternated. First you'd be drawn down into the depths, and you'd dig those holes, then you'd be yearning for heights and wide-open spaces. So you climbed onto the barn joists to get at the sparrows' nests, or onto the willow after the crows.

I was of a nervous disposition and impressionable even as a child. Whenever father showed me his belt or a whip – I dashed under the bed and lay there trembling.

"I'll teach you to climb joists! I'll show you a crow's nests! If you died straight away, it wouldn't be so bad. But you'll cripple yourself, you sonofabitch!"

And I would cower under the bed, trembling, my nose slurping, and think sadly:

'Lord Almighty! The things one has to suffer in the name of literature!'

Of the events in my early childhood which influenced my literary future, one remains firmly entrenched in my mind: a bad fall from a horse. I was galloping along on horseback through the fields when this dog suddenly bounded out from behind a grave mound. The horse lunged to one side, and I went splat on the ground! I hit the ground hard. Lay there for about an hour before I came to... I was ill in bed for three weeks after that. And then I realised that I had a calling, since I hadn't died at such an opportune moment. An unclear thought began to stir inside me then, that perhaps I was needed in literature. And so it turned out.

For those first fleeting steps of my golden childhood I was surrounded by nature on the one side and people on the other.

Later I was sent off to school.

It wasn't any ordinary school, but one belonging to the Ministry of Public Education. I was taught by a good teacher, Ivan Maksymovych, a kind-hearted old man, white as a whitewashed village house just before the Feast of the Holy Trinity. He taught conscientiously, because he was the walking conscience of the people. He's passed away now, may he rest in peace. I liked not only him, but also his ruler, which often danced over our dirty hands. It danced, because that was the 'comprehensive education system' in force then, and it always descended on our hands when it was needed, but never with great force.

Where's that ruler now, which perfected my literary style? It was the first to dance over this hand of mine, the very one now writing this autobiography. And see how well it writes? 'Like a fly breathing'. I might not have written at all, had there been no Ivan Maksymovych and his ruler that forced me to look into my books.

At this time, my 'class consciousness' began to form too. I knew already what landlords were and what the rest weren't. Father often sent me to the landlady in the manor-house with the words:

"When they let you inside, kiss the landlady's hand."

'This landlady must be quite a big shot,' I thought, 'if I have to kiss her hand.'

My class consciousness was very unclear then. Though I kissed the landlady's hand (manifest counter-revolutionary activity), I also trampled her flower beds. And once I climbed onto the veranda and pissed into the pot plants (manifest revolutionary acts).

A carbon copy of MacDonald,[36] I vacillated between socialism and the King like a wet mouse.

But even then, I was well aware of the existence of landlords.

And whenever the landlady scolded me for something and stamped her feet, I would crawl under their aristocratic veranda and whisper:

"Just wait, you exploiter of the people, till the October Revolution arrives! I'll teach you to exploit us for three hundred years..." And so on and so forth.

———•———

I was sent to school at an early age. Before I was even six probably. I studied there for three years, until I finished school. When I returned home, father said:

"You haven't had enough schooling. We'll have to send you elsewhere. I'll take you to Zinkiv, to study there a while as well, and we'll see what becomes of you."

Father took me to Zinkiv, even though they were hard times for him then, because by then there were six or seven of us, and he received only 18 to 20 rubles a month from the landlady. All the same, he enrolled me in the two-year Zinkiv Town School.

---

36   James Ramsey MacDonald (1866-1937), English political figure, co-founder of the Labour Party.

At this point, I should have turned to Neoclassicism, because I was in the same class as Mykola Zerov[37]. But I didn't want to. You know yourselves that to become a Neoclassicist requires a lot of patience. You need to read Horace, Virgil, Ovid and others of Homer's ilk. But to become a contemporary writer is far easier. No need to read anything, just sit down and write. And everyone's happy. So M.K. Zerov and I went our separate ways. He headed for Rome, and I made my way to Shenheriyevka.

I finished the Zinkiv School in 1903 with a certificate stating that I had the right to be a post-telegraph official of a very high (fourteenth or something) class.

But how could I start climbing the ladder of civil service when I was just about to turn fourteen?

So I returned home.

"You've finished your schooling early," father said. "Where will you go, given that you're still so young? I'll have to get you some more schooling, but there's twelve more mouths to feed now, apart from you."

So mother took me to Kyiv, to the Army Medical Assistants School, for father, being a former soldier, was entitled to send his children there at the expense of the government.

Off we went to Kyiv. In Kyiv, my lower jaw fell open at the station, and I went like that from the station across the whole of Kyiv to the holy Lavra, where mother and I stopped. I touched all the sacred remains, all the miracle-working icons and thaumaturgic heads, and passed the entry exams.

And so I remained behind in Kyiv. And I finished school, becoming a medical assistant.

I wasn't too bad a medical assistant, 'cause first thing I did was bathe a patient's eye in methylated spirits, instead of zinc drops.

I won't mention the reward I received from that patient.

Then a humdrum life began. I worked and studied and studied – to hell with it all! Forever an extramural student!

———•———

---

37   Mykola Konstiantynovych Zerov (1890-1941), Ukrainian scholar, professor, poet and translator. Belonged to the literary group Neoclassicists.

War overtook me at the railways, where I was bravely defending 'the tsar, the throne and the fatherland' from external enemies, assisting in the railway hospital.

When the revolution broke out, I began to rush about. Building Ukraine. Running from the Central Rada[38] to the University, and from the University to the Central Rada. Then to St. Sophia, from St. Sophia to Prosvita[39], from Prosvita to a meeting, from the meeting to a gathering, from the gathering to the Central Rada, from the Central Rada to a convention, from the convention to a conference, from the conference back to the Central Rada. There was so little time, it was frightening... I wanted to be in the army, in the parliament, the university, to be on all the committees, to collect for the National Fund and to sing songs. I was everywhere! Where there was singing – I was there! Where there were discussions – I was there! Where they conferred – I was there!

In short – I was a real statesman.

The civil war.

I took part. Shrapnel flying, me hiding... I survived the heavy burden of the Civil War. Standing in queues for rations, carting firewood by sled, digging gardens. The hardest part of it all was carrying the thirty-five kilograms of flour from the Lavra all the way to Hohol Street in Kyiv. I lugged it along the 'Dog Trail', then up Shevchenko Boulevard. Moaning and groaning and stopping and squatting. But I got it there. I didn't abandon the 'products of the revolution'.

It was hard, but 'we won'.

Well, and then a 'platform' rolled up and I was placed upon it.

Then I was freed, but I wasn't stupid, I didn't get off the 'platform'.

---

38   Central Rada – Ukrainian parliament which existed during the time of the independent Ukrainian state in 1917-1918.
39   Prosvita – a cultural-educational public organisation founded 1866, it existed into the 1940s. Its aim was the spread of education among the masses by organizing reading rooms in the villages and libraries in the towns and cities.

The book which made the greatest impression on me was Filaret's *Catechism*. What a disgusting book! If I could have read it and thrown it away, it wouldn't have been so bad. But I had to memorize it! Ah, to hell with it! It's impressed on my memory.

I've loved books ever since I was a baby. I remember when I found Solomon's *Book of Wisdom*. I sat over it for days on end, rolling a ball of yeasty bread onto that circle surrounded by various numbers. I rolled the ball until my head swam, until mother appeared, grabbed the *Book of Wisdom* and walloped me over the head with it. Only then would I stop.

In general, I preferred books with soft covers.

They were easier to tear, and not as painful when mother caught me with them.

I hated *The Russian Pilgrim*, which mother read continuously for twenty years. It was a very large book. Whenever mother took a swing at me with it, my soul dropped into my pants.

The rest of the books weren't so bad.

———•———

I began writing for newspapers in Kamianets, Podillia Province in 1919, under the name of Pavlo Hrunsky. (What was I doing in Kamianets, you ask? Same thing as you!) I began with a feuilleton.

I'm often asked where I got my language.

I got my language from my mother's tits. They were an inexhaustible well of words.

Take note of this, mothers, and your children will never have to be Ukrainized[40].

How did I perfect my language? By working. Working and taking note of the pointers of A.Y. Krymsky and Modest Pylypovych Levytsky[41], with

---

40   Ukrainization – program begun in Soviet Ukraine in the early 1920s to make Ukrainian the language spoken in the government apparatus and throughout the whole republic. Unpopular with Russians living in Ukraine and Russianized Ukrainians. Halted in the early 1930s with the demise of the semi-autonomous Ukrainian Communist Party.

41   Ahatanhel Krymsky (1811-1942), an eminent Ukrainian philologist and writer, member of the Ukrainian Academy of Sciences from 1919. Modest Levytsky (1866-1932), was a Ukrainian writer and publicist of nationalist tendencies. Pseudonyms include M. Pylypovych, Vyborny, Makohonenko.

whom I had the good fortune to work, and whom I always remember with a deep feeling of gratitude.

———•———

I lived in Kyiv. Then I was bundled off to Kharkiv in October 1920, and in April 1921 I began working for *The News* with Vasyl Blakytny[42].

At *The News* I began work as a translator. A serious job, responsible, difficult, because I had to sweat like hell over those newspaper translations.

I translated and translated and then thought to myself:

'Why am I translating, when I could be writing feuilletons? Then I could become a writer. There are so many different writers about, and I'm not a writer yet. I haven't any special qualifications. I don't know accounting, so what else is there to do?'

And so, I became Ostap Vyshnia and began to write.

I sat around and wrote. Nothing much to it, there was plenty of paper, the work wasn't very difficult – nothing as hard as copying figures into a ledger for six hours every day.

It was somewhat hard going at first, for the paper wasn't too good and the ink was of poor quality, and the pencils broke regularly, but after Knyhospilka[43] began to supply me with good stationery, things changed for the better. They even supplied blotting paper and one didn't have to press the pages of the manuscript against the wall to stop them smudging, and my writing became better and neater.

Then I bought a briefcase and became a writer of good standing.

The years passed, my seniority accumulated.

Ah, what a great thing seniority is!

It comes of its own accord, growing imperceptibly, but it provides good support.

And before you know it, seniority matures into 'stature'.

---

42 Vasyl Blakytny (1894-1925), real surname Ellansky, was a Ukrainian writer and public figure.

43 Knyhospilka – literally 'Book Union'. Ukrainian publishing and bookselling association founded in Kharkiv in 1922. Existed until 1930, and then reformed into Vukoopknyha (All-Ukrainian Cooperative Books).

When you study your hair in the mirror, you can see the 'stature' growing day by day. Very soon, instead of hair there will only be 'stature' left on your head.

Then things will go very well. You come to the editor with an article, and the editor will find it hard to refuse you. And he'll say to the secretary:

"We'll accept it! I know it's not worth a pinch of shit, but it's awkward: he's an old writer... Print it!"

And you, a man of stature, a member of the old degeneration, will say, when one of the young degeneration of writers comes to you:

"Writing is a complex craft! Once I could write! Eh, I could write! And I'd be able to write now too if it wasn't for the fact, you know, that I need to jot down my memoirs. Otherwise, I'll feel uncomfortable before history."

———

A little later that same year (1921), I began to work for *Village Truth*, where I survived five benevolent years as secretary under the direction of S.V. Pylypenko[44]. It was good working there. The paper was a fine one, God rest its soul. It loved the villagers very much. And it died from love.

———

And now a little about the creative process. How I write. I write this way. I take a piece of paper, grab a pen or a pencil, and begin writing. And write.

I always measure my temperature when I write. Normal. It's normal before I sit down to write, and it doesn't rise afterwards.

But my pulse isn't the best while I work. I can't measure it though, because when I write my hand runs across the paper and I can't grab onto an artery. And once I throw down my pen – there's no sense in taking a measurement, for it wouldn't be during the 'instant of creativity'. So I can't tell you what happens to a writer's pulse when he's writing.

As for the head during the creative process, I tried to shake my head about while writing – but this only put a damper on everything. Why this happens, I can't say for sure. The thoughts must slosh about in my head. If you place a hot teapot on your head during the creative process, you get poems instead of prose. And even these aren't very legible. If you take a

---

44   Serhiy Pylypenko (1891-1943), a Ukrainian writer and journalist.

flying leap and bash your head against a wall, then you come out with very confused *vers libre*, so that you can't understand a thing yourself.

The stomach plays quite an importart role in the creative process, too. When a person sits down to write something and writes with his right hand, holding onto his full stomach with his left, the result is a very long psychological novel, ideologically entangled. When the stomach is empty and your hand springs back because of the rumbling inside it, then usually the result will be a short iambic poem or a good short story.

When you begin to write, you must sit firmly in your chair, otherwise your head will be joined in the creative process by that part of the body from which the legs jut out. The works thus produced aren't too bad, but taking into account the exuberant growth of our culture, it's time we switched to the head.

All these observations are from my own personal experience.

A little about the influence of sexual excitation on the creative process. Some writers consider that the best works come from the pen of a person who is 'brimming' with all kinds of sexual impulses. I can't tell you how true this is. But it isn't quite right in my opinion. How can you keep abreast of 'sexual issues' when you are writing and your hand is occupied? And the head as well. In my opinion, it's hard to do. Better to stick to one or the other: either write, or create your 'sexual impulse'.

On the basis of my own experience, my advice would be: first think, then write, but not the other way around. It seems to produce better results this way, though it makes the work a little harder...

———•———

How do I view the present literary movements?

I view them. I view Vaplite, Pluh, VUSPP, Molodniak, Mars, Neoclassicists and Boomerang[45] (or whatever it's called...). I view them all.

---

45   Vaplite – *Vil'na akademiia proletars'koi literatury* (Free Academy of Proletarian Literature), a literary organisation in Ukraine 1925-28; the ideological views of its members were oriented toward European literature. Headed by Mykola Khvyliovy. Pluh – literally 'Plough', an association of Soviet Ukrainian peasant writers founded in Kharkiv in 1922. VUSPP – *Vseukrains'ka spilka proletars'kykh pysmennykiv* (All-Ukrainian Association of Proletarian Writers), literary organisation existing in Ukraine 1927-32. Molodniak – a literary organisation for Ukrainian Communist Youth League writers, founded

Eh, my dear comrades! There once lived a wise philosopher. His name was Yosyp, though I don't recall his patronymic and surname. Well that wise philosopher Yosyp once said:

"Piece of string? Let me have that too! On the road, everything comes in handy."

. . . .

Of today's writers, I like Khvyliovy and Dosvitny[46] best.

If only you knew what fine writers they are! How great it is to go hunting with them!

When morning dawns, when a silver mist rises over the estuary, when you sit in a small hide and your eyes swim through the mist seeking the distant black dot of a teal or a wild duck...

Ah!

And to your right is Khvyliovy, and to your left, Dosvitny. How can I not like them?

Especially since neither Khvyliovy nor Dosvitny ever talk about literature.

The rest are good writers too, but all they talk about is literature, and they can't shoot.

I like them too, only not as much.

Of the old writers I like Nestor the Chronicler and Ostromyr[47].

---

in Kharkiv in 1926. Mars – *Maisternia revoliutsiinoho slova* (Revolutionary Word Workshop), existed in Kyiv 1926-29, its members united by a common desire to defend literary creativity independent of Party politics. Neoclassicists – a literary group aspiring to the cult of 'pure art', with an orientation toward Western art and literature.

46   Mykola Khvyliovy (1893-1933), talented Ukrainian writer and publicist. Remained a true Ukrainian Communist and frequently launched fierce attacks against Russian intervention in Ukraine's political and cultural life. Committed suicide in Kharkiv because of harrassment by the Soviet secret police. Oles Dosvitny (1894-1934), real name Oleksandr Skrypal, a Ukrainian writer who lived in America, China and Japan, returning to Ukraine in 1918.

47   Nestor the Chronicler – date of birth unknown, but died shortly after 1113. Ancient Rus' chronicler and writer. Ostromyr was a Novgorod ruler, the viceroy of Kyiv Prince Izyaslav Yaroslavych. He commissioned the so-called 'Ostromyr Gospel'.

How do I view the theatre? I like it. I like the Berezil, Franko, Odesa and Zankovetska troupes[48]... I like them all. I even like Ukrainian opera. Cross my heart. And if the opera directors loved their operas as much as I do, despite the large numbers of our opera directors and arts section heads, we would have a flourishing Ukrainian opera. For I know that theatre is a great teaching tool, and since it is such a great tool, then we need to take a very large tool to the directors so that the theatre once again becomes a great teaching tool.

Of all the animals, I like goats the most. Of all the insects – the wasp. My favourite colour is tawny-yellow. My favourite smell, that of violets. Of all the flowers, I like fuchsias best. I like pulling cats by the tail. My favourite dish is crunchy fried potatoes. I like women shorn and shaven, and dressed in boots. I stopped believing in God two days after it was announced that He did not exist.

In addition to all this, I am a member of MODR, Aviochem, 'Away with Illiteracy', the Zmychka Society[49] and the Vasyl Blakytny Literary Club. I'm married.

That's all for the psychology of creativity.

---

48   Berezil – one of the first Soviet Ukrainian theatres to be formed, it existed in Kyiv 1922-26, and then moved to Kharkiv in 1926-33. Franko – refers to the Ivan Franko theatre troupe, named in honour of the great Ukrainian revolutionary author. Zankovetska – troupe named in honour of Mariya Zankovetska, a famous Ukrainian stage actress.

49   MODR – *Mizhnarodnia orhanizatsiia dopomohy bortsiam revoliutsii* (International Organisation for the Help of Revolutionary Fighters), a mass organisation whose aim was to provide material and moral aid to the victims of fascism, and reactionary and tsarist terror. Existed 1922-1947. Aviochem – organisation which collected money to finance aerial spraying against farm pests, such as locusts. 'Away With Illiteracy' (*Het' nepys'mennist'*) – voluntary society to help government bodies combat illiteracy, existed 1923-36. Zmychka Society – organisation taking its name from the word *zmykaty*, meaning 'to close', formed to close the gap between the village and the city. Organised travelling theatres and agitators to tour villages and keep rural folk abreast of life in the cities.

I once asked my son:

"Viachko! What do you want to be when you grow up...?"

"A person!" he said.

And I thought:

'How true. Let him be a person. Not a writer, but a person. It is easier for him to do it now than it was for me once. He won't have to kiss the land-lady's hand, and there are no potato plants or weeds around him. Nowhere to squat and think.

I've noted here the most important aspects of my life and the most important features of my nature and philosophy on life, which form the basis of my literary work. How, you may ask? What's it to you? They lie down there, so leave them be.

As you can see, the direction of my literary career was correct. And the fact that my work is worthless? That's all right. So long as the direction was correct.

P.S. Why did I hurry with my autobiography? Why am I releasing it myself? Very simple. I'm not sure that when I kick the bucket, someone will embark upon my biography... But if I write it myself, I can be sure that grateful descendants will never forget me.

Kharkiv, 15-16 March 1927

TRAVELOGUE

We'll begin traditionally, like any staff correspondent worth his salt.

The only difference being that every staff correspondent writes his impressions about a fortnight before leaving, but I had no time and I have to write now, having arrived at my destination.

I'll skip how I drove to the railway station. Firstly, it won't interest you, and secondly, I didn't drive, I actually walked, being constantly on the lookout for anyone who might swipe my bundle from the trolley. So during this time there were no impressions, apart from 'the bundle'. And a bundle is only a bundle.

Then came the impressions.

I was quite impressed by two threatening questions from a rather tough-looking woman standing on the steps of the carriage, holding a yoke in her hands.

The first question was: 'Where are you pushing?' and the second was: 'Have your eyes popped out?'

I answered gallantly that I was pushing my way into the carriage and that my eyes were still sitting in their sockets.

The woman's response to this was:

"The devil's pushing them out to here!"

But thanks to the devil I somehow boarded the carriage, was swept past five more women, and seated myself bent double on my own bundle.

By the time the third bell rang, my breathing rate had increased and my pulse had risen by twenty to thirty beats per minute.

Remembering from first aid that I still had about ten beats per minute to go, I wasn't too fazed.

* * *

Clang! Clang! Clang!

Tug!

"Oh!" (That was me).

Because I was thrown back against somebody's haunches and my neck was pressed against the woman behind me exactly on the spot just below her haunches.

And there I froze...

The woman in front of me quickly thudded down on top of me on the place just below my chest. She sat down and (may she hiccup easily) twisted about once or twice as she made herself comfortable.

Thus, the reason for my exclamation.

"Farewell, Kharkiv!' I thought.

There was a smell of sweat in the air... And milk (cow's milk, that is)... It smelled like... what didn't it smell of?

'There are many different types of smells in this world!' good old Kindrat, who died in his time from vodka, once told me.

Well, he spoke the truth.

For there really are 'many different types of smells in this world'...

Especially in train carriages, and especially when a journalist sets off on holidays.

The smells of spring...

...The woman on my chest must have been middle-class. Because I'd have snuffed it under a kulak, and a poor peasant would have been much lighter.

I groaned quietly, gently nuzzling up to the haunches of the woman behind me, while the middle-class woman on my stomach loudly husked sunflower seeds.

Outside, the rye in the fields was beautiful, the wheat ears were filling out, cornflowers played blue in the rye, cuckoos called from the woods...

Outside silver larked about in the sunflower stalks.

Outside:

> *. . . and where are the limits*
> *Which would set the sun's semesters*
> *in the azure milk of heaven?*[50]

But that was outside!

Between me and the window (I was horrified even to think!) there were some fifteen backs and a thousand kilograms of live female flesh, excluding the yokes, pots and baskets.

---

50   From Pavlo Tychyna's "In the Cosmic Orchestra" (1921).

This encounter of mine with the peasantry lasted for three stops...

The whole time I kept remembering someone's very wise words: "One must know how to skilfully approach the peasant, otherwise instead of an 'encounter' there will be a devil's carnival!"

Virtuous words. Especially 'approach' and 'skilfully'.

I was 'subjected to the peasantry', and I must say, subjected very uncomfortably and very unskilfully.

And instead of the encounter there was only the 'oh!'...

After three stops, one final smear by the wide base across my abdomen, one final bounce, and following them, my happy and joyous final 'Oh!'...

The woman got up.

Dresses fluttered past.

Someone's slender young legs suddenly landed on my liver from the top bunk. Someone grabbed me by the head and screamed:

"Will you look at this! And I thought it was a pot!"

I closed my eyes, and imagined that I was lying in the South American prairies and a herd of bison frightened by a tiger was stampeding over me...

. . . .

Later I was able to see the fields of rye for myself, and the cornflowers played azure before my eyes, nodding their small blue hats, and the fields grinned at me.

'Gone travelling, eh?'

'Why are you laughing?' I thought. 'Yeah, so I'm travelling. So what? Stop grinning...! Hasn't the same thing ever happened to you? Don't people sing about you:

> *Oh, fields, you fields,*
> *Dear mother-earth...*
> *How much blood and tears*
> *The wind has strewn upon you...*[51]

'Well, I haven't drawn any blood yet... And I haven't noticed any tears... Only... pain.'

* * *

---

[51]   Poem by Oleksandr Konysky (1836-1900), most remembered for his poem put to music "Lord, the Great and Almighty" (*Bozhe velykyi, iedynyi*).

Merefa... Yezerska... Birky...

In the carriage, there's me and another rickety old fellow who's constantly eyeing me intently. I can see he wants to start up a conversation...

Finally, he musters up the courage:

"What do you reckon – can one live without faith?"

I was thinking about my liver, about the English ultimatum, and whether wages would be increased in July.

"Of course!" I blurted out.

The rickety old fellow moved away and began to sing:

To you, the Highest warden of our lives...[52]

* * *

Bezpalivka!

End of the journey then...

And from Bezpalivka – you know yourselves – it's a stone's throw to Pasiky... As you get off the train, make an immediate left, follow the railway line a little ways, and then take a slight right and head along the road to Homilsha...

D'you know Homilsha?

"No?"

Don't you, really?! It's on the way to Pasiky! The road stretches between green meadows... As you walk along there are meadows on the right and there are meadows on the left...

If you're not sure of the way, follow the cart with your things on it...

And you'll get there...

Soon Pasiky is nearby...

There's the school up ahead...

"Trrrrr!"

We've arrived...

23.06.1923

---

52   The phrase in the original is '*Vozbrannyi uvoiedi pobidytel'naia*' and is the partially transformed text of the song praising the Virgin, which was sung in Ukrainian Churches in Church Slavonic. These songs were often learnt by ear, which gave rise to changes to the original text.

KHARKIV – KYIV

(En route)

It's all very simple.

Take five hundred and forty rubles in 1923 monetary tokens[53] (that's all) and run to the city railway station in Kharkiv.

"Kyiv, please! Express! Via Poltava."

Grab the ticket and race home.

Grab your luggage and race to the station.

Roar down the platform.

Run up to the first carriage and dash up the steps...

"Your ticket!"

"Here!"

"This is carriage seven, you're in three!"

Continue running...

Chain smoking along the way. And running from seven, in a fit of temper, toss your butt onto the platform.

"Citizen! Three gold rubles[54] fine! When will you ever learn?"

"But I... I..."

"Three rubles! Or else, please..."

---

53   In the 1920s the Soviet government tried to stabilize the currency. The first devaluation of paper money was carried out in 1921. One ruble of the new monetary tokens was exchanged for ten thousand old rubles. At the second devaluation in 1922, one monetary token ruble was exchanged for a hundred 1921 token rubles, or for one million rubles issued prior to the first devaluation. Similar monetary tokens were issued again in 1923. Banknotes were also issued from 11.10.1922 with denominations of 1,2,3,5,10 and 25*chervintsi*. In 1924 the monetary reforms were completed. Monetary tokens were phased out and replaced with rubles and copecks. 50,000 rubles in 1923 monetary tokens were exchanged for one Treasury Ruble.

54   Between 1920 and 1924 there were several currencies in circulation. Their value was continually adjusted to the value of the 1913 tsarist gold ruble. The buying power of this ruble was considered the unit to which the Soviet index was pegged.

"Ah, phew! Hell!"

"Three more rubles, citizen! Spitting is prohibited…"

Pay him only three and continue running…

"Hey, this is six! Yours is further on…"

Race up the platform.

"Yours? This is five! Keep going!"

"My God, you too!"

"Yours? This is two! You've come too far!"

"Phew! This three?"

"Yes!"

"Thank God!"

Fly up the steps. Headlong!

"Hey, what's the matter. You'll make it! What's the rush?"

"'Rush'? What's it to you? So I'm in a hurry. Think I had no reason to buy an express fare? You charge extra money for speed and won't let people hurry? What a setup!"

Plonk down in your seat…

"Go on, write!"

"I will, I will! I've been writing since I was a kid. When my hands give out, I'll use my feet!"

Clang-clang! Woo-ooh!

O-o-off we go-o-o…

* * *

The carriage is packed with Gosplan Index[55], Market Ruble[56] and 'God Almighty, a pound of white bread is eight and a half now…' types.

The corporation inspector…

---

55   At this time everyone was concerned about the Index, the arbitrary unit to which the Soviet *chervinets* and Market Ruble were pegged. The Index was set each week by Gosplan, the government planning agency, and fluctuated continually.

56   Because of the constant depreciation of monetary tokens, a so-called Market Ruble was introduced – an arbitrary monetary unit which equalled the buying power of a tsarist 1913 gold ruble. Between 1919-22 the Market Ruble was used in industry, commerce and trade in the USSR. It was used to fix wages and to assign money for government budgets.

"...Class fifteen[57], you know, plus travelling allowance... Can't complain, even though the wife's only twenty-four! I married a young one! We've a room on Pushkin Street... You from Moscow yourself?"

"Yes, from Moscow! Can't complain! The pay's one nineteen-fifteen *chervinets*[58]! Class sixteen! Fifty percent 'loading'[59]!"

"Eh! That's *kharasho*!"

"Well, and then there's the perks."

"Of course..."

. . . .

Her fingers, nails and scissors are small... She's all manicure, dressed in a cashmere skirt, with a gossamer-thin scarf right up to her chin.

"Off on holiday! For a breather! Completely worn out."

"Where d'you work?"

"Typist... Simply snowed under with work!"

"You don't look too bad!"

"I'm so tired, so tired! You're men, and we're women! It's easier for you men!"

An eye from under the gossamer scarf flashes craftily at 'you men'... 'You men' is an olive-skinned young fellow. With curly black hair... His field jacket clings to his body...

"Men and women are equal..."

"Women are more open and sincere. We trust each other! You men can't be trusted! Right?"

"And why not?"

"Because you're men, and we're women! Hee-hee! Hee-hee!"

"Sure we can!"

'Sure we can,' I thought. 'We can even be trusted...'

. . . .

"I'm in Vucoopspilka[60]! On my way to join my husband! I'm dying, simply dying! Can't wait!"

And her eyebrows shoot up. Eyebrows, what eyebrows! They'll bear

---

57   Jobs in government departments were graded from class one, the lowest, to class seventeen.

58   Until 1913, currency was issued in gold coins, thereafter it was issued as paper money. One 1915 *chervinets* equalled eight rubles in gold in 1923, and circulated during the first years of Soviet rule.

59   That is, for his normal pay, the man worked only half a day.

60   Vucoopspilka – All-Ukrainian Co-operative Union.

any weight. And so jet black! Two leeches against a white background, and straight as arrows...

"I just can't wait!"

. . . .

Koviahy... Vodiana...

Shocks and shocks of wheat...

People mowing... mowing... mowing...

Ploughing... ploughing... ploughing...

They stop, glance at the train, and again the scythe rustles through the stalks.

There'll be plenty of bread this year.

* * *

In the carriage next to mine, the budding Ukrainian opera is returning to Kyiv. The singers M.I. Lytvenenko-Volgemut, Mykysha and Lubiantsov.

Returning from a season in the capital[61].

"Well, how are things?"

"There'll be an opera. A Ukrainian opera! Everyone in Kharkiv gave us a favourable reception. We're off to Kyiv to consolidate!"

And their eyes are all glistening.

. . . .

Poltava shakes its green curls. Up on the hill there!

Here's the Vorskla River! Stalking Poltava ever so quietly, ready to embrace the city... They've been embracing a long time, Poltava and the Vorskla, madly in love with one another...

"Eh! We've got the Vorskla!"

That's the retort of a Poltavite...

"Eh! Our Vorskla flows past Poltava!"

And these are the words of those who live on the river.

Poltava stands so curly, leafy green up on the hill there, overlooking the Vorskla River.

Like a doll! So grand, grand and serene, serene and obedient.

Beautiful Poltava!

And people in Poltava are so beautiful, with such soft pronunciation.

They're not simply people, they're our countrymen...

Beautiful Poltava! Far better than Kharkiv...

---

61   Kharkiv was the capital of the Soviet Ukrainian Republic from 1919 to 1934.

Abazivka... Reshetylivka... Myrhorod...

It's growing dark in the carriage...

The corporation inspector is bringing the place down with his snoring. Smiling in his sleep. He's obviously dreaming of being promoted a class...

Miss Manicure quietly whines: 'Hush, sadness, hush,' and Miss Vucoop-spilka is making her bed and continues non-stop:

"Oh, I can't wait, can't wait!"

In the end compartment, someone has pulled out an accordion and is quietly 'reducing all executioners to dust.'

We'll reduce all executioners to-o-o dust[62]...

And the dust of the reduced executioners seems to fall into your eyes...

And... covers them...

Yank!

And the compartment is crying:

"Trindy-trindy-trindy-trindy-trindy..."

A polka!

They've reduced the executioners to dust and broken into a dance...

Dreams of dancing at a wedding all over the house with the brides-maid...

"Comrade! Steady on there! You'll bring the whole bunk down!"

'My,' you think, 'never danced in my life, and here I get carried away on the top bunk.'

A moment more... and emptiness...

* * *

"Get up, we're approaching Kyiv! The bridge is coming up!"

The train is crawling along very-very slowly...

The Dnipro River is still asleep, ensnared in a light mist...

In the distance, houses have bared their white teeth: they're being tick-led by a single ray of sunlight. Grinning, they pull the mist over themselves more tightly.

"Leave us alone! Give us a minute longer!"

Pampered little things...

---

62   A line from *The Internationale.*

The Kyiv-Pechersk Monastery...

Shooting up into the heavens with its bell-tower and stopped in mid-flight.

Maybe there's no one to shoot up toward?

And here's where they drowned the pagan god...!

Old Perun never reappeared from the water, no matter how strong he was! Drowned!

. . . .

Kyiv!

"Po-o-or-te-e-er! Faster! I'm returning home to my husband!"

"Some impatience, eh!"

28.07.1923

TELEPHONE CALLERS

I

Rr-ri-ing! (Pause) Rr-ri-ing! (Pause)... Rr-ri-ing!

That's the telephone.

"Oh, Lord! Again!" That's a busy person thinking out loud as they reach for the receiver:

"Well?!"

Then the busy person vigorously shakes their head and hastens to add into the very same receiver:

"Sorry about that, what I meant to say was 'Can I help you?'"

Someone chatters about something on the telephone to the busy person. They patiently listen, until the caller has finished, and then blurt out angrily:

"Well?!"

The busy person listens a while longer and then nervously replaces the receiver.

"Mad as hell, some people!" the busy person mumbles.

...Rr-ri-ing!

"Well?!" the same person asks, lifting the receiver. "Sorry about that. Can I help you?"

..."No, you didn't interrupt me! I interrupted myself!"

...Rr-ri-ing! Rr-ri-ing!

II

A responsible person employed in a leading government department arrives at work at nine each morning, just as they are meant to.

The person carries out responsible tasks, deciding on matters which they must study closely, and they must read lots of literature, look through countless books, in order to estimate, to compare, to weigh things in their mind, and then finally to reach a decision.

This is a person carrying out intellectual work...

Well then, the person sits down at their desk at exactly nine o'clock...
Suddenly:

"Dr-r-r-r!" The telephone.

Having answered the first call, the person opens a file and begins to read.

"Dr-r-r-r!"

"Can I help you?"

After the fifteenth 'dr-r-r!' the person no longer answers 'Can I help you?', but simply says 'Well?!' and then regaining his composure, corrects himself: 'Sorry about that. Can I help you?'

After the seventy-fifth 'dr-r-r!' the person stares at the phone for a long time, then, as if remembering something, utters 'Aha!' and picks up the receiver with the words:

"Can you help me?"

After the one hundred and eleventh 'dr-r-r!' the responsible person picks up the whole telephone, brings it to his ear and wonders:

"Gee, the receiver's become a little heavy! And it no longer fits very comfortably over my ear!"

Then the person thinks, thinks and thinks and suddenly explodes in a fit of rage:

"Hullo! Stuff you, hullo!"

And falls back into his chair.

A short while later he gets up from his chair, wanders over to the window, and looks at the glorious spring weather outside, at the bushy green linden near his window with chirpy sparrows hopping all over it...

The person looks at the sparrows, but can't remember for the life of him what these chirpy birds are called...

Then he finally remembers that they're called sparrows and becomes embarrassed at how he could have forgotten such a thing. This angers him, and he explodes in a rage:

"Someone should hang a telephone on your linden! Then you wouldn't be so chirpy!"

III

And what important business did this responsible person attend to over the telephone, without letting go of the receiver all day long?

The first callers, between about nine and ten, were very keenly interested in the health of the responsible person and how he had slept, what he had dreamt, etc.

Using all kinds of leading phrases, these morning callers tried to imply to the responsible person that they were already at work and were always punctual, and some even threw in, among other things, that to arrive at work fifteen or twenty minutes early was for them not only second nature, but also a necessity which brought them not only joy, but simply disciplinary ecstacy!

"I even bring up my children this way!" one of the callers assured the responsible person, and asked worriedly: "And how are your kiddies? People say that scarlet-fever is doing the rounds now! We have to guard our little ones! I won't let mine go to kindergarten. No! They're still children! And we're parents, so we need to act like parents!"

Dropping a few more such aphorisms, the caller crowns his call with: "Bye then! Give us a call when you have a spare moment!"

. . . .

Often they ask the person to solve difficult and high-principled problems:

"Next to the announcers' room on our floor there lives a family with children. The kids are very noisy and distract our announcers. Do you reckon we could have the family moved to another room?"

"Is there a free room?"

"Yes! Just recently vacated!"

"Then why ask me?"

"Well, you know, as they say... Heh-heh-heh! Been fishing lately?"

"I don't fish!"

"Me either! But some people fish! Heh-heh-heh! Bye!"

"Doctor of Philology Ivan Ivanovych Semicolon troubling you!"

"So you've defended your thesis already? Congratulations!"

"Yes, yes! It was quite hard! I raised a subject even Belinsky wouldn't have dared touch upon!"

"Just out of interest, what topic did you choose?"

"*The Influence of Oak Shelves on the Binding of the 1871 Edition of T.H. Shevchenko's* Kobzar."

"An interesting topic! So what's troubling you?"

"What do you think, wouldn't it be far better to write 'whoa' not simply as 'whoa', but to replace the 'h' with an apostle?"

"What apostle are you talking about?"

"Well, you know, that comma with its tail up in the air!"

"Aha! I'm sorry, but I'm not competent to comment... You'd need to approach the clergy on that one!"

"Sorry!"

. . . .

"Greetings! Greetings!"

"Who's this?"

"Didn't recognise me? During the war, don't you remember, you were on the river Elbe, and I was on the Danube!"

"Yes, I remember! There's an Elbe River and a Danube! So what did you want?"

"In the instructions it says maize should be cultivated between the rows along the length and breadth. But the Zorya Collective Farm first cultivated the crop along the breadth and then the length! Should they be taken to task?"

"Yes! Yes! Take them to task!" shouts the responsible person. "And then take yourself to task! That's all!"

IV

The telephone, they say, was invented by the German teacher Johann Philipp Reis, and perfected by the American, Bell.

They're not to blame.

Had they known that they would spawn such 'callers', they would surely have refrained from inventing the instrument.

December 1955

READ NEWSPAPERS

"Why don't you read newspapers?!"

"Why don't you keep on top of the news?"

"Why don't you know what's happening in the world?"

. . . .

"No time... Can't manage... When can there be time to read newspapers when there's so much to do... Can't do everything..."

That's one lot of excuses.

"Your newspapers don't reach us... The post is really bad... By God, it's not my fault... It's the post... Lack of transport..."

That's a second lot of excuses.

"Does your paper even come out? Amazing...! I didn't even know...!"

And a third lot of excuses.

"They just keep scribbling and scribbling there... What the hell do they keep scribbling for...? As if we didn't know ourselves what's happening... I've got heaps going on without having to worry about newspapers... Don't know why anyone would need them, anyway..."

A fourth lot of excuses.

And there are fifth, and sixth, and seventh, and forty-seventh lots of excuses...

Summarize it all, and what you have is:

"People don't read..."

Here in our parts, within a radius of 20-30-100 kilometres, people don't read local papers.

"They don't reach us, by God, they don't! It's the bloody post!"

Cunning newspaper.

Manages to reach America across various Atlantic, Pacific and Intensific oceans, but can't get to our Valky – no...

What can one do?

It's not a newspaper, more like some kind of maniac...

One needs to read newspapers, because great calamities can result from not reading papers...

I know for a fact that in this one kingdom, this one country, none of the County Executive Committees, or Parish Executive Committees or Committees for Poor Peasants ever read any newspapers...

And what happened?!

I still find it frightening...

In the County Executive Committee, in the administration department, elderberries sprouted under the chairman's desk and every time the executive committee assembled for a meeting, something would begin to grunt in the elderberries... Everyone became terribly frightened. And then two weeks later they noticed that the chairman had grown hooves.

And he tottered about on them all over the place!

And all the members of the committee began to sprout bristles on their faces.

They would assemble at a meeting and begin to grunt and oink...

Frightened the hell out of all the local folk...

So they were forced to hold fresh elections...

And meanwhile, in the parish...

The chairman there hadn't read a newspaper for ages, and it reached the point where he would dash out into the street, get down on all fours, paw the earth with his right hand and let out a bull's roar...!

They re-elected the chairman three weeks later, because the cows were going mad in their stalls...

The old grannies had begun to rebel...

In one village, the people decided:

"Why the hell do we need a newspaper? We can live happily without it!"

So what do you think happened?

The "Village Farmer" arrived with tractors for their village and found them all crawling about the fields ploughing the earth with their noses.

"We're preparing for the sowing season!" they declared in unison!

That's what happened...

. . . .

So start reading newspapers.

12.11.1922

UKRAINIZATION

An Interlude to the Play "Viy"

CHARACTERS:

1. *Head of the Ukrainization Commission*
2. *Two members of the Commission.*
3. *A young Soviet lass.*
4. *Comic figure.*
5. *A choir of seminarians.*
All characters are seminarians in disguise.

* * *

Comic Figure (*bounds onto stage and rings a bell*): Hey, pickpockets, ragamuffins, hooligans, pagans, hold your tongues! Shut up there, you ignorant runts, tone down your voices! A comedy is about to unfold here, a funny interlude.

Seminarians: Quiet! A comedy! An interlude!

Comic Figure: Rhetoricians and auditors, grammarians and brethren... The indigent, the middle classes and the wor-r-rking intelligentsia. Both Party members and those not in the Party, and even the honest non-Party members. Those who were purged and had their memberships renewed. Those 'for' and 'against'. Come on, who is 'against'? No one? That's the thing. Shut up. Hear me, hear me. Prick up your ears. We will show you how the government apparatus is being Ukrainized and explain how Ukrainization is being conducted. Listen closely and watch attentively. Remember everything we show you and make a mental note of it.

Seminarians: Hark! Ukrainization!

Comic Figure: Here comes the Commission for Ukrainization.
The Commission enters.

Comic Figure: Here comes citizen Underwood. She has been Ukrainized the full 100 % and has therefore been able to retain her Soviet job.

The young Soviet lass enters.

Comic Figure: Listen closely and watch attentively, it will come in handy, because they won't stop Ukrainizing you any time soon. Let us be attentive.

The head of the Commission quizzes the young lass. Members of the Commission record her answers. The seminarians react to all her answers with coltish "Ho-ho-hos".

Commission Head (*to lass*): Have you been Ukrainized?

Soviet Lass: Yes, already.

Commission Head: Can you please tell us why the Ukrainization campaign is being conducted?

Soviet Lass: Ukrainization is being conducted so that everyone can remain in their jobs, because if they aren't Ukrainized, they'll have to be fired.

Commission Head: Yes, yes. Tell us now, what is Ukraine famous for?

Soviet Lass (*singing*):

> *I pass through the field with my horse,*
> *Grow, oh grow, dear meadow.*

Seminarians (*suddenly pick up on the song*):

> *Take me for your bride, oh Cossack,*
> *For I love you dearly.*

Comic Figure (*clangs his bell, trying to stop the seminarians. Slowly the latter go silent*): Phew, couldn't restrain yourself, eh lads?

Commission Head (*to Soviet lass*): You wanted to give your answer in song?

Soviet Lass: But...

Commission Head: 'But' what?

Soviet Lass: In our language, that is in Russian, 'but' means "yes".[63]

The seminarians roar with laughter. Orchestra plays a flourish.

Commission Head: And what else is Ukraine famous for?

Soviet Lass: Borsch and dumplings.

The seminarians roar with laughter... Orchestra plays a flourish.

Commission Head: Well, you've learnt your Ukrainian studies well. Now we'll move onto a bit of geography... Tell us, what is a "peasant"?

---

63   She has used the Ukrainian word *ale* meaning 'but', but there is no such word in Russian.

Soviet Lass: Peasant... peasant... peasant... We weren't taught such things.

Commission Head: Weren't you? Well, but it's not all that important. Tell us, how would you say in Ukrainian: "*V vidu togo, chto...*"?[64]

Soviet Lass: *Pozakak.*[65]

Commission Head: Perfect. Perfect. You're even better than Taras Shevchenko. Tell us now, how do you write documents in Ukrainian?

Soviet Lass: All documents written in Ukrainian are begun with the words: "Given your attitude..." And in those words which had a "ye" in Russian, we simply write an "i".

Commission Head: Can you give some examples?

Soviet Lass: For example: *lyes – lis, syeno – sino, vozlye – vozli, vezdye – vezdi...*[66]

The seminarians roar with laughter.

Commission Head: All this is great. But you still haven't mentioned the most important thing. What's the most important thing in Ukraine?

Soviet Lass (*stammering*): I... I... don't know.

Commission Head: You don't know?

Soviet Lass: I don't know.

Commission Head (*to orchestra conductor*): Maestro! Jolt her memory...!

The orchestra begins to play the hopak.

Soviet Lass (*exclaims*): The hopak dance! (*And begins to dance.*)
Everyone begins to dance with wild abandon.
The Comic Figure tries to stop them. Finally, everyone settles down.

Commission Head: Fantastic! (*Continues in a solemn voice.*) Citizen Underwood, having demonstrated a thorough knowledge of Ukrainian Studies, you are transferred ex-categorically and promoted from level 10 to 14... You are free to go...

Seminarians (*singing*): Ukrainized. Ukrainized. She is Ukraini-i-i-ized.
Curtain.

1926

---

64   Russian for 'Due to the fact that...'

65   There is no such word in Ukrainian or Russian. Correct answer: *Z ohliadu na te shcho...*

66   Forest; hay; *vozle* is Russian for 'near', no such word as '*vozli*' in Ukrainian; *vezdye* is Russian for 'everywhere', no such word as '*vezdi*' in Ukrainian.

DIARY

<u>15 March 1949</u>

In any case, I wanted to note down some facts concerning the publication of my books after the war. My poor book "Antiaircraft Gun" (*Zenitka*) lay in the drawer of that swindler Rudensky (at the time he was the actual boss of the publishing house "*Radians'kyi pys'mennyk*") for two whole years. For two years Rudensky (and this means not only Rudensky, but also Stebun and co.) kept the book in his drawer. Among other things, I have this flaw in my character that I never go begging for my book or story to be published! Want to publish it – go ahead, if not – no problem! My part of the deal is only to write the thing! There are obviously people whose job it is to publish the thing, if it is worthy, to make it available to the reading public. For their efforts, these people receive a wage, etc.

So then: Rudensky kept my *Zenitka* in his drawer for two whole years. And only after Yasha Bash became director of the publishing house did *Zenitka* finally appear in print. So that in his list of works 'to be published' (in his so-called 'briefcase') Rudensky had failed to include my *Zenitka*, and had simply shoved it to the bottom of the drawer, so that the noble Yasha Bash was barely able to fish it out from there.

Why am I writing about this? Not because I've been offended by the swindler and extortionist Rudensky, or Stebun, or Sanov, but because if you start shoving Vyshnia's stuff into the bottoms of drawers, the works of a well-known author you might say, then what chance do young unknown authors have?

This was in *Radians'kyi pys'mennyk*...

What about in *Derzhlitvydav* then?! [...]

So what's the point?

There is literature, and there are writers.

There are people who publish literature: i.e. publishing houses!

For example, Malyshko, Voronko, Rylsky write some new work. They submit it to a publisher. And what do the publishers (Rozumovsky, Boretsky and their ilk) do?

They are masters of the ongoing technical process in literature...

They are the accountants as well...

And the number of poets and prose writers that one can see standing at the window of the cashier's office waiting for their honorarium... But just look at how haughtily Fira the accountant stares down at them (she, and only she!), as she counts out their money...

She may give them the money today, or she may not!

She is Fira! She's the boss of the money!

And so the poet keeps coming and coming... begging her for what is rightfully his...

What's all this about!

You might think that Vyshnia is once more denigrating the Soviet government for its terrible organization...

But why don't you think about it this way: that the cashier is acting like this on purpose, so as to compromise the Soviet government?

And this is with us writers!

So then what do they do with ordinary people?!

They are parasites (we have to finally admit that!), they are doing this on purpose to compromise the Soviet government.

And this is after they sensed that the people, the Soviet people, are not them, but just ordinary mere people!

<u>3 December 1951</u>

Glory to Gogol, Nikolai Vasylievych!

I'm translating his *The Inspector General*... How difficult this is! Di-i-i-ificult! I'll be a criminal if I turn Gogol into Vyshnia! But can I pull it off, and turn Vyshnia into Gogol?! And so we keep struggling! I want Gogol to be read in Ukrainian, just as he has the right to sound...

One Ukrainian poetess in conversation with me (we were talking about the translation of Gogol's works) asked in amazement in Russian:

"Why?"

The fact that a Ukrainian poetess asked me this in Russian did not amaze me one bit. Not at all. For she still unfortunately doesn't understand that in this world there is a folk language, a people's native language.

'Why?'

What can one say in reply?

Only one thing: here's hoping that our people don't have any more poets who utter: 'Why?'

...Back to Gogol! Nikolai Vasylievych! How can I translate him so that people love him in every village?

How? Teach me!

That poetical snob of a woman can ask in Russian: 'Why?'

It's nothing to her.

She'll earn her 10 *karbovanetses* a line for her two iambobrachs – and she'll be pleased. She can't differentiate wheat from willow: both rustle in the wind – but they'll print her poem all the same!

Which is why she can afford to say: 'Why?'

Meanwhile I must suffer on with Gogol!

I admit that it is a joyous suffering, a pleasant suffering, but all the same it is suffering!

[...]

<u>15 December 1951</u>

Gogol! I need to translate Gogol into Ukrainian! Oh, he's a hard nut to crack, that Mykola[67] Vasyliovych! What torture! It's easier to write like Gogol than to translate Gogol!

I can't do anything!

It's not turning out the way I want it to turn out. The language... that mother tongue... It simply doesn't work... The devil knows why! I'll try... But... it's just not right, not right, not right...

<u>17 December 1951</u>

Gogol again! Oh! If I could write prayers, I would pray like this:

'Lord! Let me be free of Gogol!'

And then I would add (to keep up my spirits!):

'Rejoice, O Unwedded Bride!'

And what does that mean?

Honest to God, I haven't the slightest idea!

---

67   Nikolai Gogol, a Ukrainian, was born Mykola Hohol. When he moved to Russia and began to write in Russian, he changed his name to the Russian form – Nikolai Gogol, by which he is known throughout the world.

<u>24 December 1951</u>

It's 3 am. Everyone's asleep. My wife's asleep, so is my daughter. Pavlushka, my grandson, is asleep too. Rylsky's asleep, so is Tychyna... Poetry is asleep, prose is also asleep...

Only I'm not asleep...

Why?

Because I've been told:

'Move over!'

So I'm not asleep! I'm chewing on Gogol! Yes, I'm chewing on Gogol!

Mykola Vasyliovych has caused me much grief. That he has! I think that if M.V. Gogol had known that his work was going to be translated into Ukrainian he would have written his 'comments' to *The Inspector General* somewhat differently...

He is so furious, so angry, that...

And we have to make head or tail of it! Well, spit in my face, reproach me, torment me, scream at me, but I will say all the same: 'Gogol could have written his comments to *The Inspector General* far more competently. I will defend my words before all Gogol scholars, Gogolomaniacs, etc.

I'm no linguist by any stretch of the imagination. I'm no expert in Russian either, but I am a reader, who can, to a certain degree, compare the Ukrainian language with Russian...

[...]

<u>12 February 1952</u>

So I've finally finished translating Gogol's *The Inspector General*. I was greatly aided (a big thanks to him!) by M.T. Rylsky.

A perfect job?

Of course not!

One needs to work one's whole life on the translations of the works of Gogol in general, and especially *The Inspector General*, to make them close to the original.

But how are things normally done in our country?

Hurry, hurry, hurry...

And there you have it...

[...]

<u>23 February 1952</u>

I'm translating *In the Foothills of Mount Ararat* – a musical comedy. I have this feeling that I'm taking part in a criminal act.

And that I'll be tried in court for 'aiding and abetting'...

And they'll convict me!

And rightly so!

[...]

<u>23 February 1952</u>

They say my translation of *The Inspector General* is good.

That's what they write!

My God! I'm ashamed! One needs to spend one's whole life translating Gogol!

But without dictionaries!

Without the help of all those Dashkeviches et al...

How nicely Mykola Vasyliovych can be presented in our Ukrainian language!

It only needs a bit of hard work!

You can't do it the way it was with me: 'Quick! Quick! C'mon! Hurry up!'

If it wasn't for Rylsky, I would have 'c'moned' something terrible!

<u>25 March 1952</u>

I'm translating this musical comedy from Russian into Ukrainian. I won't mention the authors. There are two of them!

Experience shows that:

a) shit, no matter in which language it is written – will never turn into gold by way of translation. Shit is shit in any language.

b) but a good thing written in a foreign language can be turned into shit by a shitty translator.

How about that!

ORIGINAL TITLES
OF TRANSLATED WORKS

A Jack of All Trades – *I VUTsVK, i Radnarkom, i Derzhplan, i UER, i...i...* First published in *"Visti VUTsVK"*, 5 July 1925.

An Alternative – *Al'ternatyva*. First published in *"Visti VUTsVK"*, 25 September 1925.

Berlin's Museums – *Berlins'ki muzei*. First published in *"Visti VUTsVK"*, 31 July 1928.

Blue Bog – *Synia triasovyna*. In *"Usmishky"*, vol. 4, (1930, Kharkiv), 51-58.

Breed More Goats – *Poshyrennia kozy sered naselennia*. First published January 1922

Carp – *Korop*. First published 26 July 1951.

Chauvinism – *Shovinizm*. First published in *"Trudova hromada"*, 1 January 1920.

Choose One of Your Locals – *Vyberit' kohos' iz mistsevykh*. First published in *"Visti VUTsVK"*, 3 January 1925.

Cooperative Matters – *Spravy kooperatyvni*. First published in *"Visti VUTsVK"*, 29 October 1925.

Crimean Moon – *Kryms'kyi misiats'*. First published in *"Visti VUTsVK"*, 30 May 1924.

Crimean Nights – *Kryms'ka nich*. First published in *"Visti VUTsVK"*, 29 May 1924.

Crimean Sun – *Kryms'ke sontse*. First published in *"Visti VUTsVK"*, 15 June 1924.

Diary – excerpts from *"Dumy moi, dumy moi..."* (Shchodennykovi zapysy)

'Down With Shame' – *"Het' sorom"*. First published in *"Visti VUTsVK"*, 3 October 1924.

Guard the State's Wealth – *Berezhit' dobro derzhavy*. First published in the newspaper *"Radians'ke selo"*, 8 April 1926.

Gynaecology – *Hinekolohiia*. First published in "*Visti VUTsVK*", 23 July 1925.

Hard Times – *Kruti chasy*. First published in "*Visti VUTsVK*", 14 February 1925.

How I Went Fishing – *Iak ia rybu lovyv*. First published in "*Visti VUTsVK*", 30 May 1923.

How Sad – *Sum obhortaie*. First published in "*Selianyn*", 29 October 1925.

How to Cook and Eat Wild Duck Soup – *Iak varyty i isty sup iz dykoi kachky*. First published in "*Perets*", 1945, iss. 5-6, 13.

How to Get Through Customs – *Iak pereikhaty mytnytsiu*. First published in "*Visti VUTsVK*", 9 September 1928.

How to Improve Your Household – *Iak polipshyty svoie hospodarstvo*. First published in "*Visti VUTsVK*", 7 July 1925.

Kharkiv-Kyiv (En Route) – *Kharkiv-Kyiv (Dorohoiu)*. First published in "*Visti VUTsVK*", 28 July 1923.

Making Money – *Sprytnist'*. First published in "*Visti VUTsVK*", 12 February 1926.

Market Day – *Iarmarok*. First published in "*Visti VUTsVK*", 25-31 July 1925.

Misfortune – *Hore*. First published in "*Visti VUTsVK*", 3 March 1925.

Mountains – *Hory*. First published in "*Visti VUTsVK*", 8 June 1924.

My Autobiography – *Moia avtobiohrafiia*. In "*Usmishky*", vol. 1, (1930, Kharkiv), 7-24.

My Merry Galosh – *Kalosha smialas'...* First published in "*Visti VUTsVK*", 31 October 1925.

Our Qualified Graduates – *Teoriia bez praktyky*. First published 13 July 1923.

Read Newspapers – *Chytaite hazetu*. First published in "*Visti VUTsVK*", 12 November 1922.

Searching Kharkiv for a Tractor Yard – *Iak ia v Kharkovi "trakhtornoho dvoru" shukav*. First published in "*Visti VUTsVK*", 28 August 1925.

Sheep Breeding – "*Vivcharstvo*". First published in "*Selians'ka pravda*" 5-6 August 1925.

Snipe – *Bekas*. First published in "*Dnipro*", 1945, iss. 10, 71-81.

Summer by the River – *Pliazh kyivs'kyi*. First published in "*Visti VUTsVK*", 31 July 1923.

Telephone Callers – *Dzvonari*. First published in *"Perets"*, December 1955.

The Beach – *Pliazh*. First published in *"Visti VUTsVK"*, 1 July 1924.

The Best and Surest Way of Becoming Rich – *Prekrasnyi i naipevnishyi sposib zabahatyty*. First published in *"Visti VUTsVK"*, 1 November 1923.

The Clubhouse – *"Klub"*. First published in *"Selians'ka pravda"*, 8-10 March 1925

The Corruption of the Bourgeoisie – *Rozklad burzhuazii*. First published in *"Visti VUTsVK"*, 18 July 1928.

The News (1921) – *"Visti" 1921 roku (Tini predkiv nezabutykh)*. In *"Usmishky"*, vol. 4, (1930, Kharkiv), 35-39.

'The Sexual Problem' – *"Polova problema"*. First published in *"Visti VUTsVK"*, 4 April 1924.

Those Ukrainian Peasants! – unable to verify source or original title.

Tourists – *Turysty*. First published in *"Visti VUTsVK"*, 27 May 1924.

Trading in Air – *Povitriam torhuiut'*. First published in *"Visti VUTsVK"*, 12 July 1924.

Travelling Abroad – *Poikhaly...* In *"Tvory v semy tomakh"*, vol. 4, (1964, Kyiv), 208-212.

Travelogue – *Podorozhni vrazhennia*. First published in *"Visti VUTsVK"*, 23 June 1923.

Tried It? – *Sprobuvav?!* First published in *"Radians'kyi selianyn"*, 1925, iss. 19, 36.

True Christians – *Spravzhni khrystyiany*. First published in *"Visti VUTsVK"*, 12 July 1924.

Ukrainian Studies – *Deshcho z ukrainoznavstva*. First published in *"Visti VUTsVK"*, 27 April 1923.

Ukrainization – *Ukrainizatsiia*. In *"Usmishky"*, vol. 3, (1928, Kharkiv), 226-229.

Upkeeper of Morals – *"Nravstvinna robota"*. First published in *"Vsesvit"*, 1926, iss. 11, 2-3.

The Selected Lyric Poetry
Of Maksym Rylsky

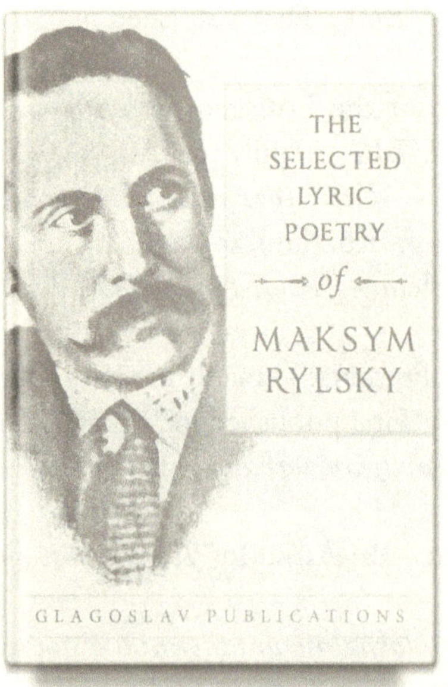

Maksym Rylsky (1895-1964) is one of the most outstanding Ukrainian poets of the the 20th century and master of the genres of the modern sonnet and the long narrative poem. He was closely associated with the Neoclassicist group of Ukrainian poets, who employed traditional poetic forms with rhyme and meter, wrote in a clear and accessible contemporary idiom, and often referenced Ancient Greek and Roman mythology as well as numerous other authors from world literature in their poetry. Rylsky was also a prolific translator from English, French, German, and Polish as well as a folklore and literary scholar, who worked most of the earlier part of his life as a teacher of philology.

Buy it > www.glagoslav.com

Maybe We're Leaving

by Jan Balaban

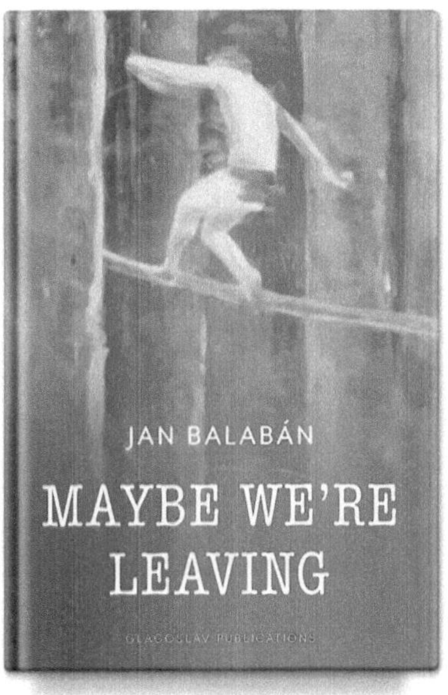

A young boy from the housing estates comes across a copse of old oaks to which he can escape, as to an oasis of calm. Although he may forget about it once he becomes an adult and "puts aside the things of childhood," it will remain a locus of balance, decades later, for a single mother struggling with the difficulties of raising the child she loves. A husband, on the lip of an ugly divorce, drives across town in the middle of the night to rescue his wife, abandoned by her lover, and then — as she falls asleep in the car — takes the long way home, to prolong a moment such as he has not experienced in years. An elderly doctor, self-diagnosed with Alzheimer's disease, makes use of the few precious moments of consciousness granted him each morning to pass on to his grandson what he has learned about life and living responsibly. Loss, and permanence, the ephemeral and the eternal, are common themes of Jan Balabán's collection of short stories Maybe We're Leaving, presented here in the English translation of Charles S. Kraszewski. With psychological insight that rivals the great novels of Fyodor Dostoevsky, the twenty-one linked narratives that make up the collection present us with everyday people, with everyday problems — and teach us to love and respect the former, and bear the latter.

Buy it > www.glagoslav.com

Acropolis – The Wawel Plays

by Stanisław Wyspiański

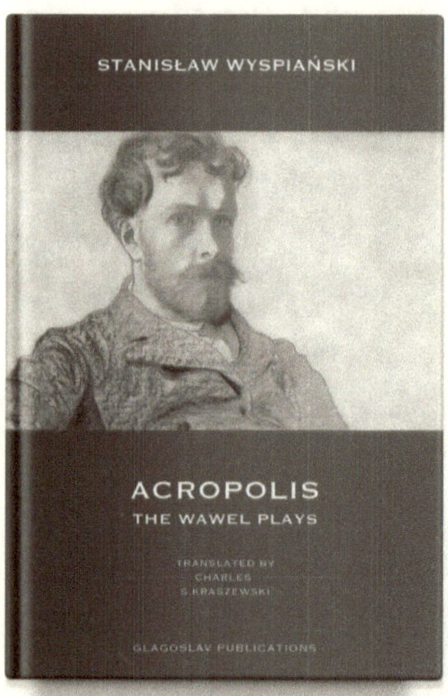

Stanisław Wyspiański (1869-1907) achieved worldwide fame, both as a painter, and Poland's greatest dramatist of the first half of the twentieth century. *Acropolis: the Wawel Plays*, brings together four of Wyspiański's most important dramatic works in a new English translation by Charles S. Kraszewski. All of the plays centre on Wawel Hill: the legendary seat of royal and ecclesiastical power in the poet's native city, the ancient capital of Poland. In these plays, Wyspiański explores the foundational myths of his nation: that of the self-sacrificial Wanda, and the struggle between King Bolesław the Bold and Bishop Stanisław Szczepanowski. In the eponymous play which brings the cycle to an end, Wyspiański carefully considers the value of myth to a nation without political autonomy, soaring in thought into an apocalyptic vision of the future. Richly illustrated with the poet's artwork, *Acropolis: the Wawel Plays* also contains Wyspiański's architectural proposal for the renovation of Wawel Hill, and a detailed critical introduction by the translator. In its plaited presentation of *Bolesław the Bold* and *Skałka*, the translation offers, for the first time, the two plays in the unified, composite format that the poet intended, but was prevented from carrying out by his untimely death.

Buy it > www.glagoslav.com

Dear Reader,

Thank you for purchasing this book.

We at Glagoslav Publications are glad to welcome you, and hope that you find our books to be a source of knowledge and inspiration.

We want to show the beauty and depth of the Slavic region to everyone looking to expand their horizon and learn something new about different cultures, different people, and we believe that with this book we have managed to do just that.

Now that you've got to know us, we want to get to know you. We value communication with our readers and want to hear from you! We offer several options:

– Join our Book Club on Goodreads, Library Thing and Shelfari, and receive special offers and information about our giveaways;

– Share your opinion about our books on Amazon, Barnes & Noble, Waterstones and other bookstores;

– Join us on Facebook and Twitter for updates on our publications and news about our authors;

– Visit our site www.glagoslav.com to check out our Catalogue and subscribe to our Newsletter.

Glagoslav Publications is getting ready to release a new collection and planning some interesting surprises — stay with us to find out!

Glagoslav Publications
Email: contact@glagoslav.com

Glagoslav Publications Catalogue

- *The Time of Women* by Elena Chizhova
- *Andrei Tarkovsky: The Collector of Dreams*
  by Layla Alexander-Garrett
- *Andrei Tarkovsky - A Life on the Cross* by Lyudmila Boyadzhieva
- *Sin* by Zakhar Prilepin
- *Hardly Ever Otherwise* by Maria Matios
- *Khatyn* by Ales Adamovich
- *The Lost Button* by Irene Rozdobudko
- *Christened with Crosses* by Eduard Kochergin
- *The Vital Needs of the Dead* by Igor Sakhnovsky
- *The Sarabande of Sara's Band* by Larysa Denysenko
- *A Poet and Bin Laden* by Hamid Ismailov
- *Watching The Russians (Dutch Edition)* by Maria Konyukova
- *Kobzar* by Taras Shevchenko
- *The Stone Bridge* by Alexander Terekhov
- *Moryak* by Lee Mandel
- *King Stakh's Wild Hunt* by Uladzimir Karatkevich
- *The Hawks of Peace* by Dmitry Rogozin
- *Harlequin's Costume* by Leonid Yuzefovich
- *Depeche Mode* by Serhii Zhadan
- *The Grand Slam and other stories (Dutch Edition)*
  by Leonid Andreev
- *METRO 2033 (Dutch Edition)* by Dmitry Glukhovsky
- *METRO 2034 (Dutch Edition)* by Dmitry Glukhovsky
- *A Russian Story* by Eugenia Kononenko
- *Herstories, An Anthology of New Ukrainian Women Prose Writers*
- *The Battle of the Sexes Russian Style* by Nadezhda Ptushkina
- *A Book Without Photographs* by Sergey Shargunov
- *Down Among The Fishes* by Natalka Babina
- *disUNITY* by Anatoly Kudryavitsky
- *Sankya* by Zakhar Prilepin
- *Wolf Messing* by Tatiana Lungin
- *Good Stalin* by Victor Erofeyev

- *Solar Plexus* by Rustam Ibragimbekov
- *Don't Call me a Victim!* by Dina Yafasova
- *Poetin (Dutch Edition)* by Chris Hutchins and Alexander Korobko
- *A History of Belarus* by Lubov Bazan
- *Children's Fashion of the Russian Empire* by Alexander Vasiliev
- *Empire of Corruption - The Russian National Pastime* by Vladimir Soloviev
- *Heroes of the 90s - People and Money. The Modern History of Russian Capitalism*
- *Fifty Highlights from the Russian Literature (Dutch Edition)* by Maarten Tengbergen
- *Bajesvolk (Dutch Edition)* by Mikhail Khodorkovsky
- *Tsarina Alexandra's Diary (Dutch Edition)*
- *Myths about Russia* by Vladimir Medinskiy
- *Boris Yeltsin - The Decade that Shook the World* by Boris Minaev
- *A Man Of Change - A study of the political life of Boris Yeltsin*
- *Sberbank - The Rebirth of Russia's Financial Giant* by Evgeny Karasyuk
- *To Get Ukraine* by Oleksandr Shyshko
- *Asystole* by Oleg Pavlov
- *Gnedich* by Maria Rybakova
- *Marina Tsvetaeva - The Essential Poetry*
- *Multiple Personalities* by Tatyana Shcherbina
- *The Investigator* by Margarita Khemlin
- *The Exile* by Zinaida Tulub
- *Leo Tolstoy – Flight from paradise* by Pavel Basinsky
- *Moscow in the 1930* by Natalia Gromova
- *Laurus (Dutch edition)* by Evgenij Vodolazkin
- *Prisoner* by Anna Nemzer
- *The Crime of Chernobyl - The Nuclear Goulag* by Wladimir Tchertkoff
- *Alpine Ballad* by Vasil Bykau
- *The Complete Correspondence of Hryhory Skovoroda*

- *The Tale of Aypi* by Ak Welsapar
- *Selected Poems* by Lydia Grigorieva
- *The Fantastic Worlds of Yuri Vynnychuk*
- *The Garden of Divine Songs and Collected Poetry of Hryhory Skovoroda*
- *Adventures in the Slavic Kitchen: A Book of Essays with Recipes*
- *Seven Signs of the Lion* by Michael M. Naydan
- *Forefathers' Eve* by Adam Mickiewicz
- *One-Two* by Igor Eliseev
- *Girls, be Good* by Bojan Babić
- *Time of the Octopus* by Anatoly Kucherena
- *Soghomon Tehlirian Memories - The Assassination of Talaat*
- *The Grand Harmony* by Bohdan Ihor Antonych
- *The Selected Lyric Poetry Of Maksym Rylsky*
- *The Shining Light* by Galymkair Mutanov
- *The Frontier: 28 Contemporary Ukrainian Poets - An Anthology*
- *Acropolis - The Wawel Plays* by Stanisław Wyspiański
- *Contours of the City* by Attyla Mohylny
- *Conversations Before Silence: The Selected Poetry of Oles Ilchenko*
- *Nikolai Gumilev's Africa* by Nikolai Gumilev
- *Zinnober's Poppets* by Elena Chizhova
- *The Hemingway Game* by Evgeni Grishkovets
- *The Secret History of my Sojourn in Russia* by Jaroslav HašekCharles S. Kraszewski
- *Mirror Sand - An Anthology of Russian Short Poems in English Translation* (A Bilingual Edition)
- *Maybe We're Leaving* by Jan Balaban
- *A Brown Man in Russia - Perambulations Through A Siberian Winter* by Vijay Menon
- *Death of the Snake Catcher* by Ak Welsapar
- *Duel* by Borys Antonenko-Davydovych

More coming soon...

www.ingramcontent.com/pod-product-compliance
Lightning Source LLC
Chambersburg PA
CBHW050403190726
48284CB00007BB/2402